CW01647473

The Parents' Room

By

Susan Dodd

Grosvenor House
Publishing Limited

This book is published by
Grosvenor House Publishing Ltd
Link House
140 The Broadway, Tolworth, Surrey, KT6 7HT.
www.grosvenorhousepublishing.co.uk

A CIP record for this book
is available from the British Library

ISBN 978-1-80381-585-5

Dedication

Just for Judy
and
absent friends...

...and thanks to Greta's family for
allowing me to use her name
and photograph.

Contents

CHAPTER 1

Memories

I stood in the room.
It was quiet and eerily silent.
The air was clear and clean –
Not at all how I remember it.

I can picture them all now… ghosts from my past, each and every one of them still capable of bringing a smile to my face, and a tear to my eyes, even after all these years. Oh, how they could sometimes drive you to the brink of despair, and then give you a feeling of pride, joy and achievement. No other job could command such a yo-yo of emotions.

I sat down in the solitary old familiar, easy chair in the empty room, closed my eyes and wandered off into the echoes of the past. The overwhelming smell of cigarette smoke drifted back, and the loud chatter, clinking of mugs and noisy children filled the room. The room was alive again and I was back.

I had first arrived in the Parents' Room over 20 years ago. It was based in the Meadows Infant and Nursery School on the Meadows Estate.

The sprawling estate comprised mainly of council houses, framed by privately owned properties, with long winding avenues and a web of smaller roads snaking off them. Some areas were run down with uncared for gardens, and plastic bags caught in overgrown hedges. The occasional pushbike was propped up against a wall, and stray dogs wandered around. In contrast, there were nicely painted and cared for properties, with tidy gardens, neatly mown lawns and smart cars parked in drives. My first visit to the Parents' Room was just before the school broke up for the summer holidays. I was due to take up my position in September at the end of the holiday – the start of the new school year. The Head Teacher, Mrs Harper, had walked with me across the school hall and into the Parents' Room.

She was a very elegant lady with an impeccable dress sense. Having said that, she was very down to earth with a mischievous sense of humour. I had only met her a couple of times, but I already knew that I liked her.

"It's bingo this afternoon, so the room will be full. They take their bingo very seriously," she chuckled.

Alarm bells rang – I had already heard about interrupting bingo sessions!

I was feeling a little nervous as I entered the Parents' Room for the first time. A fog of smoke hit me, and I was conscious of several pairs of eyes looking slightly indignantly in my direction.

"Sorry to interrupt everyone. This is our new Community Teacher, Sally Brown," explained Mrs Harper, "she has come to meet you all so I shall leave her in your capable hands," and with that, and a smile of encouragement, she went on her way.

"Shift up Carol and let the lady sit down," barked a gruff voice with a faint Scottish accent. "I'm Greta and I run the bingo among other things. Do you want to play? We've only just started and it's only £1 a book."

"Er, yes please, I'll give it a go," I stuttered nervously.

Fumbling in my bag I found £1 and handed it over.

"These are your cards and this is your dabber," replied Greta, and a sudden warm smile crossed this older lady's rather weather-beaten face, with a ciggie hanging from the corner of her mouth.

"Thanks," I answered, smiling back.

I instinctively knew that I had to make friends with this particular lady. I took my place in the allotted space next to Carol. No one else said a word – they just looked.

"Right, eyes down for a line across or down, corner to corner, or the four corners and the middle," instructed Greta.

"Got that duck?" asked Carol, poking me with her dabber.

"Shush," hissed a few people.

I nodded to Carol, who gave me the thumbs up, and a toothy grin.

The games came and went, and the concentration was intense as ciggies were being puffed with great determination. Eventually, it was the big prize – a meat hamper! As Greta called out the numbers, I realised that I was dabbing mine off at an alarming rate, and soon I needed only one number – 22.

"Please don't," I prayed to myself.

"Two little ducks – 22," called out the Scottish twang.

My heart sank, my courage failed me, and the meat hamper was lost. I didn't say a word and continued to pretend to dab! To this day, I still have two matching Santa candles that I had won at a later date playing bingo. I display them every Christmas on my fireplace, and when I take them out of the box, they always make me smile.

Some people would question what a teacher was doing playing bingo in the afternoon – it was part of the job to play 'the bingo' very occasionally.

The role of the Community Teacher carried a wide range of duties, the main one being the running of the Parents' Room within the school. The Room consisted of a large table surrounded by second-hand saggy chairs and a small sofa. There was a sink with a water boiler, a double kitchen unit with cupboards and a Baby Belling cooker sitting on the flat shelf along with a microwave. There was an extractor fan which alleviated the smoky atmosphere until it became too tired with over work! The school holiday flew by, and September came along with the start of the autumn term, and the first day of my new job. I had had fifteen years of teaching relatively well behaved four to eight year olds, and I realised that working with adults, who could answer back, was going to be a very different experience.

I arrived at the Parents' Room in good time, only to find that Greta was already there.

"Morning Sal. Thought I would get in early for your first day," she said, with the usual ciggie hanging from the corner of her mouth.

"Thanks Greta, that's very kind of you," I replied with a smile and a surge of relief. I had an ally here. Her weather-worn face was framed by frizzy, brown dyed hair with flecks of grey showing through. Glasses which looked as though they had seen better days, bordered her brown eyes.

"Here, drink this, they'll all be arriving soon," she said, thrusting a mug of strong coffee towards me.

"Any tips?" I asked.

"Yes! If you play the bingo again and win, make sure you shout," she replied with a grin.

We both burst out laughing.

"How did you know?" I asked.

"It was the look of panic on your face," chuckled Greta.

"What's so funny at this time in the morning?" asked a gravely voice, followed by coughing.

"Want a drink Carol?" called Greta, as Carol parked a buggy in the small entrance to the room

"Yes please, tea if you are making it," came the reply, as Carol entered the room carrying a little girl of about ten months old.

Carol had wrinkly skin, making her look older than her years. She had yellow, nicotine-stained fingers which were a testament to all the ciggies she had smoked. Faded blue eyes peered out from under a straggling light brown fringe, along with an endearing toothy smile. As I got to know Carol, I realised sadly, that she lacked confidence and needed constant reassurance.

Her little girl, Chloe, was the product of an alcohol-fuelled 'bloody good night out' – father unknown.

"Oh God, is the kettle on? I need a coffee," croaked a pretty young woman with a mass of curls, and an hourglass figure, and two young daughters in tow.

"Been on the piss again Casey?" enquired Greta, handing over a mug.

"Yeah – don't remind me," groaned Casey. "I feel real shitty."

I was to discover that Casey and her partner Ian, both liked a drink and it was becoming a problem.

"Come on in Sara, come and meet the new teacher. It's Sal isn't it?"

"Yes, that's me," I replied. "How are you?"

"I'll be okay soon," Casey smiled. "I never learn. This is my cousin, Sara," she continued.

I soon learnt that Sara was a painfully shy, single mum who had a baby called Maisie. Unfortunately, Sara had suffered badly from a break up with her partner, and had developed agoraphobia. With Casey's encouragement she could now walk down the school path to the Parents' Room where she felt comfortable and safe. She relied on her family and friends to do all of her shopping for her.

"Hi Sara, good to meet you," I said quietly.

Sara just nodded and sat down in a corner of the room, with Maisie on her knee. The room gradually filled up with mums, dads and children waiting for the bell to ring. Greta was producing mugs of coffee as if they were on a conveyor belt. I was most impressed.

"Don't expect this service everyday," she announced, "and please don't forget to wash your mugs before you disappear."

The school bell rang out and there was a mass exodus from the room.

"MUGS," shouted Greta, making me jump. "I'm not your skivvy!"

Despite the warning a few managed to escape without washing their mugs, leaving Greta muttering obscenities under her breath.

As the week went on, I got to know most of the regular visitors to the Room. There was Emma, who had a mop of unruly black hair, and very dark brown eyes framed by long, luxurious eye-lashes. She was always bemoaning the fact that her backside looked too big in her leggings.

Then there was Abbey, who was always quiet and pensive. She had long, brown hair hanging down like curtains at the side of her face. Sometimes she would sit with her head down and her hair drawn across her face as if to say "keep out, I'm not here today".

Janine was a regular visitor. She had a daughter Keeley, who was four years old, and a son Adam, who was eighteen months old. She was rather a large lady who seemed to find everything an effort. Little Adam was always plonked on the floor with a few toys and left to his own devices. This often resulted in him throwing his toys around and tearing up books – he had no respect for people or things around him. This was not his fault – he didn't know any better and Mum didn't help. I quickly picked up the vibes that this annoyed other participants in the room.

There were also the dads who used the room, one of whom was Pete. His wife Chris had just been diagnosed with breast cancer. Pete came across as a helpful, caring man who was worried sick about Chris and wanted to do his best for her.

We were just settling down on the Wednesday morning to listen to a talk about the library and books for the children when the phone rang in the room. It was Wendy, the school secretary.

"Hi Sally, Mrs Harper would like you to go on a home visit."

"Okay," I replied. "I'll come and get the details. See you later folks – I have to go out."

"Where are you going?" asked Carol. "I bet it's to the new lot in The Grove. They're a mucky bunch."

"Stop being a nosy mare," retorted Greta. "here, drink this and shut up," she continued, handing Carol a mug of tea, almost dropping some ciggie ash into it, "and no sloping off at dinner time without washing the mugs. I'm getting fed up with doing it all, again."

After getting the details from Wendy, I set off for The Grove. It was my first home visit and it felt odd leaving the building. Carol was right – I was visiting the 'new lot' although I would never admit that to her.

Zoe, the little girl in the family had only attended school for one day, and my job was to find out why. I drove round the maze of roads, waving to a few people on the way. I pulled into The Grove and parked in the corner outside the house I was visiting. Although car crime was rather prevalent on the estate, I never worried about my car. I always knew that it was being 'looked after' wherever I parked it. I knocked on the grubby, blue front door, and looked at the rubbish strewn across the garden – such a contrast to the property next door with its smartly painted cream door and carefully planted shrubs.

The door opened a crack.

"Yes? What do you want?" said a gruff voice, followed by a chesty cough.

"I'm Sally Brown from school. We were wondering if everything is alright with Zoe, as she has only been to school once so far."

"Better come in and see the missus duck," said the voice.

The door opened and revealed a chubby, red-faced man dressed in a murky looking vest and baggy tracksuit bottoms.

I followed him through a very untidy and smelly kitchen and into the lounge.

"She's from school and has come to see why our Zoe hasn't been going," he explained to two women sitting on a saggy, brown settee. Also sitting there was a young boy of about two years old with a blue dummy stuck in his mouth. He had grey eyes, blond hair and a runny nose.

"That's our Zoe's mum," the man said, pointing to a plump person with black matted hair, and dressed in purple tracksuit bottoms and a pink shirt, "and that's Granny," he continued, pointing to the other woman.

Granny was of equal, ample girth with grey, fuzzy hair, round, dark rimmed glasses with thick lenses and pop socks covering her chubby ankles.

"Sit down duck," the man said, pointing to an equally saggy chair. "Granny, make the young lady a drink."

"No really, no thank you," I protested, but Granny had already disappeared into the kitchen. Oh dear – too late!

"Zoe's upstairs. She's been a bit upset," explained Mum, looking decidedly uncomfortable.

"A bit upset," repeated Granny, emerging from the kitchen with two mugs of tea.

She put one on the table next to me, and passed the other, which had World's Greatest Lover printed on it, to Dad.

I glanced down at my mug and could not believe my eyes. Floating on top of the tea were baked beans, and the rim of the mug was covered in congealed fat! My stomach recoiled in horror.

"Do you know what's bothering Zoe?" I enquired, frantically trying to put the vision of the tea out of my mind.

By now, they were all sitting on the settee listening intently to me, and their eyes firmly fixed in my direction.

"Could be Twinkle," replied Mum.

"Could be," echoed Granny, eyeing me through the thick lenses.

"Twinkle?" I asked, "who is Twinkle?"

"Over there," nodded Dad. "in the cage."

I looked over at the cage, and there was a brown and white guinea pig lying on its back, with its legs sticking up in the air. Twinkle was obviously not twinkling any more, judging by the amount of flies around the cage.

"Not moved for days," murmured Mum, twisting a strand of straggly hair round her little finger.

"For days," copied Granny.

"Was Twinkle Zoe's pet?" I gently enquired.

"Yes, that's right. She loved Twinkle," replied Mum, wiping a tear from her cheek.

"Loved Twinkle," came the echo.

"Well I think it would be a good idea if you moved Twinkle and buried her in the garden, then Zoe may not be so upset," I advised.

"Good idea duck," said Dad. "I'll do that. Don't know why I didn't think of it."

"Goodness me, is that the time?" I exclaimed looking at my watch, "I must get back to school."

I grabbed the mug, picked up my bag and raced into the kitchen. I emptied the contents of the mug down the sink without stopping and bid a hasty farewell.

The next day I was pleased to see Zoe back in school.

The library talk had gone down very well, especially with Casey who loved books, and she had tried her hand at writing poetry.

Pete requested a talk about breast cancer and everyone thought it would be a good idea.

As the weeks went by, I realised that I would never know what each day would bring, or who would walk through the door.

CHAPTER 2

Miles Apart

I was soon bound-up in my new job and I loved it. Parents usually came to visit the Room just for chat and a cuppa, whilst others came to join in the Adult Education classes that were running. For others it became a haven where they could be offered support and guidance in their often traumatic lives. For a few, it was an escape to leave their problems at home – at least for a while.

One of the main aims of the Room was to promote good parenting, and to raise self-esteem and self-worth. To say that some of the occupants had low self-esteem was an understatement.

The Room was a hive of activity from 8.30 in the morning until going home time. Early mornings were always chaotic, and the kettle would go into overdrive as parents arrived for a cuppa and a ciggie before the bell sounded for the children to go into school. Prams cluttered the small outer room, making it an obstacle course for people wanting to get into the Parents' Room. Latecomers would have to leave theirs outside in the garden, and would grumble if it was raining. We had our fair share of tiffs and falling outs, but somehow, laughter always won through in the end.

The Adult Education Classes varied - Maths, English, Sewing, Cooking and talks about any subjects that the participants asked for – within reason. Life ticked along comparatively quietly....for a while. Casey joined the Adult Education English class, and was developing her poetry and creative writing skills.

We were very lucky to have a good relationship with the senior schools in the area, and they were happy enough to share their facilities with us. Once a week we went swimming, played badminton and had games of netball. It was so rewarding to see busy mums (and dads) having 'their time', and growing in confidence.

Following Pete's request for a talk about breast cancer, the day for the talk arrived. Several parents stayed to listen, including Pete. The woman giving the talk duly arrived and set up her screen for the slide show of her visual demonstration.

I noticed that she barely acknowledged any of the parents in the room, and I thought that I saw the occasional look of disdain flicker across her rather less than friendly face, as she chatted to the ladies and Pete. I knew that their language was not to everyone's taste, but it was certainly not outrageous – most of the time! As the time approached for the talk to begin, the woman began to look anxious and flustered.

"Is everything alright?" I enquired.

"I don't know. Is that man over there going soon?" she replied.

"Pete? Oh no, he has come because his wife has breast cancer, and he thought that this would help him to understand more about it," I explained. "Is there a problem with that?"

A red flush appeared on the woman's neck.

"I can't possibly give the talk and slide show with a man present."

"Why ever not?" I enquired in amazement.

"It just would not be appropriate," she retorted, "especially here, on this estate."

I felt my hackles rising. What did I have here?

"I can't ask him to leave, it's not right," I responded as quickly as I could, not wanting an uncomfortable situation to arise.

"Well, that's easy – you don't ask him to leave, you tell him," came the haughty reply.

"Is there a problem?" asked Pete, picking up on the conversation.

An unhappy murmur rippled round the room, and I could feel the hostility and icy indignation setting in.

I glanced at Greta, who raised her eyebrows as much as to say, "right Sally, we must defuse this situation."

Greta was going from strength to strength. She understood the people who lived on the estate, and I was learning so much from her.

"She thinks that you have just come to look at the titties Pete," cracked a voice from a corner.

There were a few sniggers and, for the first time, I swung round and glowered at Carol. I didn't say a word – I didn't need to!

"I thought that if I came to this talk, it would help me to understand and teach me how I could support my wife and family better," said Pete quietly. "Are you saying that I can't stay because I am a man?"

"Quite right," sniffed the woman, turning away from Pete.

"I can tell you what this is about," continued Pete, his voice breaking with emotion. "You are embarrassed because I am a man who happens to live on an estate that you clearly do not like. People like you think that we don't have feelings. Well, let me tell you this – we do have feelings just like anybody else, and I guess that I am the first man who wanted to come to one of your talks and you cannot handle it!"

The room was silent for a change and you could have heard a pin drop.

My mind was in a whirl. Do I tell this snobby woman to sling her hook and deprive the mums out of a valuable talk – or what? I had to think on my feet. I took a deep breath and decided.

"I do feel that you are being unreasonable," I commented as calmly as I could, "and I feel that if you are not prepared to go ahead if Pete is here, then you should be the one to leave,"

I felt a hand on my shoulder – it was Pete.

"No Sally, I'll go. It's not fair to spoil it for everyone, and put you in an awkward situation."

"Thanks Pete, I owe you one," I replied, looking into his steely grey eyes that could hardly conceal his fury as he turned to leave.

"Cheers Pete," called several voices from the room. Pete raised a hand in acknowledgement – or did I see two raised fingers?

The talk went ahead, albeit in a very frosty atmosphere, but I should not be asking that certain woman back again. Pete was a much bigger and better person than she was. I could not believe that someone in such a position could have such an obvious bigoted view about the people who live on the Meadows Estate.

My heart went out to Pete who, despite his humiliation and fury, retained his dignity. I felt myself being emotionally drawn, and a unique, close bond was being formed with the people of the estate.

CHAPTER 3

New Horizons

Sewing classes as always were very busy. Casey was planning her wedding to her long-term boyfriend, and boozing partner, Ian. There was great excitement as she was making her wedding dress in the room. The paper dress pattern was carefully pinned onto the delicate, cream, lacy material she had chosen, with a satin lining to match. Casey wanted everybody to be involved in her wedding plans, and each person in turn was cutting out a piece of the dress. Greta even put the ever-present ciggie well out of the way when it was her turn.

"Your turn now Sal," said Casey, turning to me.

"Frigging hell! You're not letting Sal loose on your dress are you?" chuckled a voice from a corner. "you should have seen the mess she made cutting some material for a table cloth."

"Thanks for reminding me of that Carol," I replied, smiling. "Cheeky! This material should go well against your dark complexion Casey."

"Thanks," she replied beaming and tucking her shoulder length mass of golden curls behind her ears."

Casey handed me the pinking shears with a confidence I certainly did not feel.

"This is the last piece of the sleeve to cut, Sal," explained Jane, the sewing teacher, "and then everyone here has played a little part."

I picked up the shears and inched them towards the delicate material. As I was just about to make the first cut, there was a loud strumming.

"Drum roll," shouted Carol, as she began to bang her hands on the window sill.

"Carol!" yelled Casey, "go and play with the traffic outside if you are going to be so bloody daft!"

"Oooh, I beg your pardon, sorry I spoke," muttered Carol with a toothy grin.

"You will be if you ruin my dress," retorted Casey.

"Okay, no harm done. Let's all calm down so that I can cut this beautiful material without making a mess of it," I said.

Pushing my blond hair out of my eyes, I took a deep breath and began to cut around the pattern. Except for the ticking of the clock there was silence in the room. All eyes looked expectantly in my direction, and it felt as if everybody was holding their breath. As I cut round the final corner of the pattern, there was an audible sigh of relief, and I thought that I saw a glint of a tear in Casey's eyes.

"Thank you," she whispered, "now everybody has had a turn."

As I mentioned earlier, we had good relationships with the local senior schools, and the mums really enjoyed playing netball.

"How about having a netball team and taking on other schools that have a Parents' Room?" suggested Lizzie, a freckle faced, keep fit nut.

This idea was met with much enthusiasm, so I set about making enquiries. The mums practised very hard and took it all very seriously. In the sewing classes they made their own red tabards with the position machined on, using black tape so they were ready for their first match. They were rather naughty when they played a "fun match" against the staff from the next door junior school. Somehow they had managed to stretch cling film across the goal into which the staff were shooting in the first quarter!

After playing a couple of local games I was running out of options, so I was delighted to receive an invitation to play against a Parents' team from 'across the river'. We set off early in cars so that we would be there in good time for the start of the match. The ladies were in high spirits as we left Meadows Infant and Nursery School, and were looking forward to the events of the morning, and going somewhere different for once. Casey was her usual bouncy self, and Emma was bemoaning the fact that she had bought a size too small in leggings, and that her backside was way too big. She had tied her mop of unruly black hair into a pony-tail, and her very dark eyes were framed by those long, luxurious eye lashes.

Abbey, on the other hand, was rather quiet and pensive. This did not unduly bother me as she was always rather shy and withdrawn. She loved playing netball and had really gained in self-confidence since joining the group, and was coming out of her shell. From little snippets of conversation I had heard, I suspected that she lived with a partner who always put her down, and did not allow her to be herself. Her long, brown hair covering her face hung down as usual.

To reach our destination we had to drive over the new suspension bridge crossing the river. On the approach to the bridge, we were all admiring the stunning view in front of us. The sun was catching the water, making its gentle waves shimmer as the bridge rose majestically to span the wide stretch of water below. I glanced in my mirror and realised that I could only see Emma's reflection.

"What's going on? Where's Abbey?" I enquired, feeling rather puzzled.

"She's lying on the floor," came Emma's matter of fact reply.

"Why?" I spluttered.

"'Cos she's scared of the water and this is the first time she has been out of town – ever!" explained Emma, "didn't you know?"

I could not believe what I was hearing.

"No, I had no idea. Why didn't she tell me?" I asked.

"I did try but you were always so busy, and I felt daft," came a smothered answer from the floor of the car.

I felt so guilty. I remember Abbey coming to talk to me on a couple of occasions, but each time I had asked her if it could wait until another time, as I was due to go out on home visits – I never got back to her! A lesson had been learned – if people came to talk to me, there was obviously a good reason for it, and I must take it on board. What an effort it must have been for Abbey, as she would not have wanted to let the netball team down. As it was, it was actually me who had let her down.

"Abbey, I am so sorry," I cried. "I should have made time for you."

"It's okay. I've made it. Are we over the water yet?" came a shivering voice.

"Yes, get up now and get that seatbelt on before we go through to toll booth," encouraged Casey. "We don't want Sal getting into trouble. We'll look after you."

"Okay, okay. I'm still shaking like a leaf," answered Abbey, appearing ashen faced in the mirror.

She clipped her seatbelt back on, and brushed back her long, brown hair. My mind was still in a whirl but I had to concentrate on my driving. We went down a tree-lined avenue with huge houses on each side.

"Wow! Look at these dream houses," whispered Abbey, "I've never seen any like those before."

"We've got some big houses like those back home in our town," replied Emma, "haven't you seen them?"

"No. I don't go into town," confessed Abbey. "Jack goes if I want anything that I can't get from the shops on the estate. My mum never went into town either."

I could hardly believe what I was hearing. How could this be happening in this day and age? How many more people were living like this?

We soon arrived at the school, and now I had to concentrate on the netball match.

"You okay?" I just managed to ask Abbey before the ladies went to get changed.

"Yes, do you know, I am?" she replied smiling. "Thank you."

"What for?" I asked, amazed

"Well, if it wasn't for you, I wouldn't be here," came the answer as she skipped off after the rest of the team.

I felt tears prick the back of my eyes. Sometimes, I felt very humble.

We drove back on a high. We had won the match and had had a lovely time meeting the other mums from the opposing team. They had made us all feel so welcome. As for Abbey, she sat in the front seat next to me, and took in all the sights around her. She even kept her eyes open going back across the bridge. I suspect that a whole new world was about to open up in front of her.

As soon as we arrived back at the Meadows, they all bustled into the Parents' Room to tell the others of their success, and I went to tell Mrs Harper about the match. She was always interested in what the parents were doing, and was very keen to hear about Abbey.

Not all of the members of staff were enthusiastic about the Parents' Room. One or two of them could not understand the concept behind it and wondered 'why we bothered' with those people. If they had joined in and made an effort to get to know them, then they would have realised 'why we bothered'. It was interesting to note that it was always these teachers who had the most disputes with the parents.

I wandered down the corridor looking at the children's cheerful artwork displayed on the boards. Sometimes, I missed working with the children – they didn't answer back and question things like the adults I work with now.

"Sally, have you a minute please?" called Mrs Harper from her room as I walked past. I turned round and went back to the Head teacher's room.

Doreen, who was in her fifties, and her daughter, Lisa, in her early thirties, were there with their social worker Jill. Doreen had care of two of Lisa's five children, and the other three were in foster care.

Lisa was the children's mother but she was not cut out for motherhood however much help she was given. Doreen and Lisa were always at loggerheads over something, and today was obviously no exception. They were glaring at each other, and if looks could kill then they would both have been dead.

"Hi Jill, good to see you," I said, smiling at the social worker.

"You too," came the reply. "We seem to have the same old problem. Doreen and Lisa are arguing again, and the children are stuck in the middle as usual. I have been trying to explain to them that it is just not good for the children to be in an atmosphere like this. It is obvious that the two of them are poles apart."

Doreen screwed up her wrinkled face, peered over her ill-fitting glasses, and looked puzzled. She shook her head which was swathed in a silky red and blue headscarf, which was covering her rollers, except for one that was protruding and wobbling out from under her scarf. Doreen had a speech impediment and at times it was difficult to understand her.

"Don't be so duddy faft!" exclaimed Doreen, "our pardens back on to each other, so how can we be soles apart. Bloody stupid woman!"

I daren't look at Mrs Harper, as I could feel laughter building up in my stomach, and we shared the same sense of humour.

"Doreen, please don't be so rude," I said, as sternly as I could.

"Okay, porry," muttered Doreen, scowling at me over her glasses.

"What I meant was you are not close and are miles apart," spluttered Jill.

"Piles apart now are we?" cried Doreen. "You don't know what you are palking about. We live near each pother you daft prat. Tome on Lisa. I'm not listening to this fload of crap any more."

With that, Doreen and Lisa flounced out of the room and, for once, they were united. Lisa didn't say a word and the door closed with a bang. Doreen could be heard chuntering all the way down the long corridor.

"Didn't handle that very well, did I," exclaimed Jill.

We all looked at each other and it was time to fall about laughing – which we did!

Some you win and some you don't, and that was one of them.

I found my way back to the Parents' Room and found Cassie sitting in the armchair in the corner looking rather dejected.

"You look fed up," I commented.

Her spiky, dyed blond hair was gelled upright, and her heavily made up eyes stood out from her slightly 'squashed' face.

"Yea. Hubby's coming home early on leave from the army, but my boyfriend hasn't gone out on the trawlers yet, and he is still at home."

No answer to that one really, and not one to get involved in.

Carol was busy cooking stew and dumplings, helped and encouraged by everyone in the room. Carol didn't think she could do anything well, and was so proud of herself for attempting to cook. Janine was slouched in a chair with her nose stuck in a magazine. Adam as usual was sitting on the floor, when he suddenly launched a toy car that narrowly missed Chloe and landed in Carol's stew.

"It's about time you got that frigging kid of yours under control," shouted Carol. "that car nearly hit Chloe and it landed on my dumplings."

"Well, if you don't want them, pass them over and I'll eat them," retorted Janine sullenly.

"I'll stuff it where you don't want it if you're not careful," scowled Carol. "you should get off your fat backside and watch what Adam is doing, instead of sitting there and ignoring him. It's not fair on Adam. We raise money to buy books and toys for the kids to use in here, and all Adam does is wreck them and you don't seem to care."

This was quite a speech for Carol and she went red in the face with embarrassment when she realised that the room had fallen silent and everyone was listening to her.

"She's right you know Janine, we are all fed up with it," commented Casey. Other heads nodded in agreement.

The bell for dinner brought the tense situation to a close. Janine escaped with Adam and went to the Nursery to collect her daughter, leaving all the toys scattered over the floor.

They were rather conspicuous by their absence for a couple of days, and I was thinking that I would have to do a home visit when I got the surprise of my life. Walking into the Parents' Room after lunch I found Adam sitting on the floor playing with the car mat and beside him was Janine. I tried not to look amazed, but I couldn't conceal my delight.

"Hi Janine, nice to see you," I exclaimed.

Janine glanced at me and grinned shyly.

"It's good this – playing with your kid. I had got so wrapped up in my own problems, I forgot what I really should be doing," she commented. "the girls were right to have a go at me. I'm sorry I've been a pain in the arse, oops backside."

I felt a real warmth for this young mum.

"Let us help you if we can," I said quietly, "that's what we are here for."

"Yeah, I know, but it's hard to admit that you are struggling to cope," Janine answered with tears glistening in her eyes. "Look at me crying, I never cry. I always got told off if I cried, and then got a slap or a punch to make it worth crying for."

The floodgates opened and I was pleased that we were on our own. Whether I should have done or not, I put my arms round Janine and hugged her. She cried enough tears for the whole of her heart wrenching childhood. From that day onwards, she embraced the concept of the Parents' Room. Gradually, she talked about the horrors of her upbringing, with a cruel father who had to be obeyed, and a mother who was too scared to protect her from regular beatings with a belt. She drew strength from the girls in the Room as they sympathised and supported her. I did ask if she wanted to talk to a trained counsellor but she declined. Janine had grown in self worth and confidence just by sharing her dreadful experiences.

As a follow up to a library talk, a visit to a nearby library was arranged. Casey was very enthusiastic as she had never been in a library before.

It was a lovely, crisp autumnal morning as we set off to walk to the library. Chloe and Adam were both tucked up in their pushchairs.

"Did you ever run through the leaves when you were little Sal?" asked Casey, as we were passing the park at the top of the road.

"Yes I did, many times. I loved the sound the leaves made," I replied, smiling at the memory.

"I wasn't allowed to in case I got mucky," sighed Casey, wistfully.

I glanced at my watch.

"Look, we don't have to be at the library yet, so do you want to give it a go now? We've got plenty of time," I suggested, half jokingly.

Casey paused for a moment, and a huge grin enveloped her face.

"Okay, let's go for it girls," she cried, startling a passer-bye on a bike.

Adam and Chloe were helped out of the pushchairs and stood holding hands, wondering what to do.

Casey was rushing through the leaves kicking them with her feet.

"Come on Carol," she called, "it's fun"

"No, I feel a twat," muttered Carol. "People will think I'm stupid."

"Not if you hold Chloe's hand and show her what to do," I answered. "go on."

She hesitated for a few seconds and then took hold of Chloe's hand and began to stamp and kick the leaves.

"Me, me," shouted Adam, running to Janine and pulling at her coat.

Without further ado, mums and children were laughing and shrieking with enjoyment. I had to chuckle along with them – such joy at such a simple pleasure.

"Time we were going," I called after about ten minutes of cavorting among the leaves,

"At least the leaves were dry" commented Janine. "It would have been a bit embarrassing if we had turned up at the library all muddy."

Adam and Chloe were strapped back in their buggies and we continued on our journey.

"Yoo hoo, wait for me," called Greta as she trundled along behind us, pushing a shopping trolley.

"I forgot all about the library visit," she puffed, catching up with us. "I've got the bingo prizes in the trolley. I hadn't got time to go back to school with them, so I've brought them along with me. Goodness, what have you been doing? Your faces are glowing like smacked babies arses!"

"Just running amongst the leaves. Adam and Chloe wanted to," replied Casey, quickly, with a ghost of a grin on her face.

"Let's get a move on," I intervened before Carol could argue about who wanted to play in the leaves.

We arrived at the library and found the rest of the group there.

Hazel, the librarian, greeted us warmly. She did look a bit bemused when Greta parked her shopping trolley containing the bingo prizes in the foyer.

Casey's eyes widened when she saw all the books, especially when she found some poetry books.

"Haven't you been in a library before?" I enquired quietly.

"My mam said it wasn't for the likes of us and I believed her," she whispered sadly.

Hazel asked the group what they thought would improve visits to the library for them. They made several sensible suggestions, but the overriding comment was a better understanding from library staff for mums with noisy children!

CHAPTER 4

Christmas Comes

Christmas was approaching and discussions began in the Parents' Room about the Christmas dinner. There were cries of "where's the pen?" when a sheet of paper, decorated with bells and holly, was stuck to the wall for people to add their names if they wished to attend the festive event.

Christmassy name cards began to circulate in the Room and nearby Nursery, getting more and more frantic as the dinner approached. Greta was in charge of fund raising events and she took the job very seriously. If you poked your nose into the Room, or were in shouting distance, you did not escape her attention at this time of year – not even an unsuspecting Ofsted Inspector who ventured across the smoky threshold. I don't know what impressed him most, the length of ash hanging from Greta's ever present ciggie, or her well endowed son Andy prancing around in figure hugging Lycra gold tights, as he practised his role for the Christmas pantomime. It was a very quick inspection of the Parents' Room! We did however, receive excellent feedback!

Numbers for the dinner soon reached thirty five and the list was closed. The shopping list was in progress, and decisions were yet to be made as to who was preparing and cooking what. Chocolate logs were well under way in the Thursday morning adult education classes. Plastic leaves and robins were in abundance and could be found anywhere in the room. Finished items were placed high on every available shelf and fiercely guarded from determined furniture-climbing toddlers who could smell chocolate.

Casey's half-finished wedding dress was put safely out of harm's way until after the festive season. There was no rush to get it finished, as the wedding was not until the summer.

Cooking and vegetable preparations were allocated – Casey was stuffing and cooking the turkey at home, Pete was in charge of the pigs in blankets (his wife Chris was recovering from breast cancer and was looking forward to the dinner), Emma was preparing the vegetables and the roasties, and Greta and I were making trifles instead of Christmas pudding.

I was at home putting the final touches to my trifle when I received a phone call from Casey.

"I have just remembered that we said we would put a small chicken on as Carol can't eat turkey," she spluttered. "Sorry Sal, can you get one and cook it please? I am up to my armpits in stuffing, and I've had a few cans of lager."

My heart sank as I was just on my way to the night football match, and I was already running late.

"Okay, no worries," I replied, "I'll call at the supermarket and pick one up."

"Thanks Sal. Back to the stuffing," she chortled. "See you tomorrow."

I shook the last few chocolate sprinkles onto my trifle and popped it in the fridge. Grabbing my hat and coat, I dashed to the car. Rushing into the supermarket I grabbed a small chicken out of the freezer and hurried to the checkout. I could not miss the kick-off – that would be sacrilege.

The chicken paid for, I took off at speed through the checkout and promptly slipped and fell flat on my back. The frozen chicken shot out of the carrier bag and hurtled down an aisle like a ten-pin bowling ball and disappeared in the distance.

Feeling rather winded, and blinking at the lights on the ceiling, I tried to gather my senses. The face of a young male shop assistant loomed over me. He was obviously trying to keep a straight face!

"Where's my chicken?" I spluttered, as he helped me to my feet.

"It went that way madam," he replied, pointing down the aisle, his face getting redder and redder. He finally dissolved into hysterics – who could blame him? I joined in the laughter with him as we retrieved the chicken several metres away from where I fell. Luckily, my chicken didn't floor any of the OAP's and my football team won.

Did it really matter that I was cooking a chicken at gone eleven at night? I can't re-call if cooking chickens or making trifles were in my job description.

Christmas dinner day dawned, and I set off for school wearing my snowman Christmas jumper. The chicken and trifle were carefully balanced in a box in the car boot. I carefully negotiated the jumble of pushchairs and toys in the entrance lobby and, with a sigh of relief, I arrived in the Parents' Room with my food contributions towards dinner, safely intact.

The room was packed and the smoke extractor fan was working overtime. I glanced around the seemingly chaotic scene and then I realised that it wasn't. Janine was sitting in the corner armchair, with a group of children around her as she read a Christmas story.

Emma was finishing off preparing the vegetables, and the remainder of the food was being placed on the large table for later. Greta was guarding the crackers from the odd stray child who was attracted by the shiny, bright colours of the wrappers.

The school bell rang and the children were ushered across the hall to their classrooms and into the Nursery.

"Right! Let's get cracking. We've a lot to do," announced Greta. "Carol, can you go to the classroom and set the tables?"

"I'll just finish my fag and then I'll go," replied Carol.

Greta frowned and peered over her glasses at Carol.

"Alright, just the one. I know you young lady," grinned Greta, putting festive paper tablecloths, plates, dishes, cups and crackers on the chair next to Carol.

The morning grew more and more frantic as lunchtime drew closer. The turkey was being sliced, the vegetables were being put into containers ready to be warmed up in the microwave, and Pete was cooking his pigs in blankets in the Baby Belling oven.

As midday approached, the guests began to arrive and were ushered into the spare classroom for lunch. With five minutes to go, Carol wandered back into the Room.

"Greta, they want to know what they are eating their dinner with," she announced.

"Frigging hell Carol, You've been over there all morning. Didn't you realise that there was no cutlery and didn't think to tell me?" exclaimed Greta in exasperation.

"I thought that they might be bringing their own," replied Carol, without batting an eyelid.

Greta looked at me and rolled her eyes.

"It's okay. I'll nip down to the kitchen and borrow some. I'm sure it will be fine," I said

"Sorry. My fault. I forgot about knives and forks," confessed Greta. "Sorry Carol, I didn't mean to shout."

"No probs," replied Carol, grinning, "I'll let you off."

A happy buzz filled the air as crackers were pulled, jokes read out and party hats were put on, and everyone had a knife, fork and spoon! The army of volunteers carried the food as quickly as they could to the 'dining room', where there was a line of helpers waiting to serve the guests whilst it was still warm.

It still amazes me to this day how a full Christmas lunch was served to so many people with so little equipment.

The Christmas festivities were not complete without the traditional visit from Father Christmas to deliver presents to the young children at the dinner, even though several of them ended up howling with fright and hiding behind their mums. Greta beamed with pride as her son Andy posed as Father Christmas, resplendently dressed in red, complete with white hair and beard, and black boots.

Carol chuckled out loud.

"What's tickling you?" asked Greta.

"I prefer him in the gold Lycra tights," cackled Carol.

"Don't you mention those tights, it's embarrassing," cried Greta, joining in the laughter, her weather beaten wrinkles turning into smiles.

Weird and wonderful costumes appeared in the Room as the parent's Christmas panto approached. It didn't matter that they hardly ever turned up to rehearsals as long as they had an impressive costume to wear. Somehow, with a great deal of ad-libbing and me as the narrator they always managed to put on a show that the children loved. I don't know what the rest of the teaching staff thought about it all – I never dared to ask.

Snow White and the Seven Dwarfs was this year's production. There were pointy hats, tunics and stripy tights draped everywhere, along with cardboard picks and shovels covered in silver foil. Greta was playing the wicked queen and looked formidable dressed in black, with a long cape and hood. Her son Andy was playing the prince and still insisted on wearing the clingy Lycra tights, much to his mum's horror. He only agreed to wear a cloak to cover up his modesty when it was pointed out to him that some of the older children, being children, might find things funny and laugh, not to mention the staff. This was much to Greta's relief, and mine, not that I wanted to dampen anyone's enthusiasm.

Casey was Snow White and Abbey, Carol, Lizzie, Emma, Janine and two others were the Seven Dwarfs. Pete was the huntsman looking very dashing in his costume and wearing a feather in his cap. The Dwarfs were applying blusher to redden their faces.

As usual, the children filed into the hall for the performance, and there was a frantic last minute panic in the Room.

"Where is it?" shouted wicked queen Greta.

"Where's what?" I asked.

"My poisoned apple to give to Snow White," she exclaimed.

"Do you mean the apple that was near the cooker?" enquired Carol.

"What have you frigging well done with it?" choked Greta.

"I've eaten it. I thought it was a spare one," chuckled Carol.

"It's not funny," shouted the usually calm Greta, "what am I going to do without an apple?"

"I've got a banana," offered Casey.

"Banana?" spluttered Greta.

"If it's going spare, I'll have it," said Andy, spinning round in his golden tights.

"Don't even think about it," stormed his mum, "and stop twirling!"

"Think about what?" asked Andy, with a wicked grin on his face.

"I'll go and borrow a plastic one from the Nursery," said Casey, "they play with them in the shop."

"Put that banana away before you go," instructed Greta, with a ghost of a smile flicking across her face.

Casey dashed off to the Nursery and managed to borrow a plastic apple, and relative calm returned to the Room, with the banana nowhere in sight.

The children laughed and cheered at the sight of their parents in costume. As usual, my heart was in my mouth hoping for no major disasters. It was so lovely to see them throwing heart and soul into the panto and not caring about looking silly. I was amazed and proud at how some of them had grown in self-confidence in such a short space of time. They gave each other encouragement and support, and learned to laugh at themselves. For some of them, I knew it was an escape from often difficult lives, and for a while it was 'their time'.

The dwarfs were making their final entrance and I was just beginning to relax. I then realised that only six of them had appeared – who was missing? Suddenly, the door flew open and in dashed Carol – playing Doc.

"You daft gits. You left me behind," she shouted. "I hadn't got my bloody beard on."

"Stop bloody swearing," hissed wicked witch, Greta.

For a second there was silence and everything seemed to freeze in time. All of a sudden, the dwarfs started to sing.

"Heigh ho, heigh ho, it's off to work we go," at the top of their voices as they waved their picks and shovels.

The children didn't seem to notice, and some members of staff were obviously trying not to laugh. Others looked po-faced as if to say "what did you expect?"

The panto ended to rapturous applause and the parents took their bows proudly. Andy could not resist doing a quick pirouette as he left the hall. Carol had quickly disappeared, and I returned to the Room to find her curled up in a chair, sobbing her heart out.

"I let you all down, and I let myself down," she gulped. "I am so sorry."

I hesitated for a moment, wondering how to answer her. In a way she was right, but I didn't want to knock her new found confidence. The door opened and in came my saving grace. It was Lauren, one of the Nursery staff.

"Carol you were great. That was hysterical," she exclaimed laughing.

"I shouldn't have sworn," sniffed Carol.

"No, maybe not, but I don't think many of the children picked it up," said Lauren. "Anyway, many of them will have heard much worse at home! Just think, a few months ago, you wouldn't have dared to take part in a pantomime – you should be very proud of yourself, young lady."

Carol managed a watery smile as the rest of the cast returned to the Room.

"Oh Carol, that was so funny," chuckled Andy, doing yet another triumphant twirl in his golden tights. "The other teachers have said how much they enjoyed the play – well most of them. There are always some who have no sense of humour."

Carol beamed a toothy grin, and put her beard on and wiggled round the room singing.

"Heigh ho, heigh ho, it's off to bloody work we go. Happy Christmas everybody."

CHAPTER 5

Contrasting Lives

Christmas faded into a distant memory and the spring term began. Casey continued sewing her wedding dress with great care and pride as it slowly took shape. Guest speakers came and went and the particularly popular ones were keep fit, relaxation, health and beauty.

We had several informal discussions on topics such as childhood illnesses, children not sleeping at night, marital problems, money management and too many more to mention.

The Parents' Room was always busy, with new people coming and friendships flourishing. I was kept busy trying to help them with various problems that arose, such as those with the electric and gas boards, council house matters and other very personal situations. Sometimes I felt that I had helped and at other times I was not too sure. On some occasions no advice would be taken and the bad situations just continued. Very frustrating, but people have to make their own decisions and take the responsibility for their actions. I didn't judge them, I just tried to show support wherever I could. Casey's cousin Sara was becoming a regular visitor to the Room and was very slowly gaining in self-confidence.

"Do you know what I should really like to do, Sal?" she said one quiet day.

"What's that then?" I enquired,

"I should love to have Maisie baptised," she replied.

"What a great idea," I answered.

"Yes I know, but there is no way I can go to church," Sara said, sadly. "I know I can't."

I looked at Sara's grey, tear filled eyes, and realised just how much this meant to her. The school had a good relationship with the local vicar, and an idea was forming in my mind.

"How about if we could baptise her here in school?" I said, quietly.

Sara's eyes widened with delight, and a smile engulfed her round face.

"Oh wow! That would be amazing," she cried.

"I shall have to speak with Mrs Harper and the vicar about it, so don't get too excited about it yet," I chuckled at her delight.

As I knew she would be, Mrs Harper was delighted and enthusiastic about the idea, and luckily, Reverend Metcalf was equally so.

It was decided that the whole school would come to the baptism, along with people that Sara wished to invite. Casey volunteered to choose Maisie's baptism dress, and Sara sent out invitations to her family and friends. The gang from the Parents' Room was invited as a matter of course.

A little while before the exciting event, Sara came and sat next to me in the Room.

"Sal, can I ask you something?" she whispered.

"Ask away," I whispered back.

"Would you be one of Maisie's Godparents, please?" she asked timidly.

For once, I was so taken aback that words failed me. It was so unexpected.

"I should be delighted," I replied when I had recovered myself.

"Thanks, that means a lot to me," said Sara, warmly.

The school hall was brightly decorated with children's painting and work. Reverend Metcalf had constructed an alter with church drapes over tables, and a mobile font with a silver container of water. She was resplendent in her full church robes. Parents and friends soon filled up the chairs at the back of the hall, and they were followed by the children who sat in front of them.

Maisie looked cute in her white dress, matching tights and shoes. She had a white bow perched in her hair.

I and the other Godparents, took our places near the alter with Sara, Maisie and Reverend Metcalf. The service started with the singing of 'Morning has Broken', led with gusto by Mrs Harper. Maisie looked rather startled by the sudden noise, and then kept the children amused by bouncing and waving in her mother's arms.

The children settled down and listened with great interest as the vicar conducted a very simple baptism service. I found myself feeling quite emotional as we Godparents said our vows. Maisie chortled as the water was splashed on her head, making everybody smile. The service finished with the singing of 'Lord of the Dance'.

As the children left the hall, they chattered excitedly about what they had seen and had been part of. I think that many of them would remember this experience for a long time.

When we returned to the Parents' Room there was another surprise that even I didn't know about.

Organised by Greta, the parents had all chipped in and put on a lovely spread. One clever mum had made and decorated a beautiful pink and white cake. Reverend Metcalfe and all the visitors were invited, so the Room was soon at bursting point. Sara was quite overcome by the attention and could not believe what they had done for her, and I knew then without a doubt why 'I bothered' with these people.

(By the way, I have watched my Godchild Maisie grow up into a wonderful young lady, who now has a baby of her own. Maisie is so proud to be able to tell people that she was baptised in a school.)

The following morning I was despatched off on a home visit to find out why six year old Marty, always seemed to be so tired at school, even first thing in the morning. The curtains were all drawn at the house, despite it being half past ten. I walked tentatively up the path making sure that the barking dog next door, couldn't get out.

"Shut that dog up," a voice yelled from somewhere. I knocked sharply on the door and waited. There didn't seem to be much sign of life. My hand was just about to knock again when the door opened. A dull-eyed, drowsy looking woman dressed in black, silky pyjamas peered round the door.

"Yeah? What is it?" she drawled.

"I'm Sally from the school, Mrs Sinclair. Please may I have a word with you about Marty?" I asked. "May I come in for a minute?"

Without a word she turned and I followed her, shutting the door behind me. The atmosphere was very dark and heavy, and a sweet smell hung in the air. In the dull light of the lounge, I could see that the furniture looked classy and expensive. As I sat down, Mrs Sinclair lit up a ciggie and breathed in, deeply.

"Well, what's up?" she enquired, scowling.

"We are rather worried that Marty is always tired at school, even first thing in the morning. Doesn't he sleep very well or does he go to bed late?" I asked, my eyes beginning to smart in the smoky atmosphere.

"Funny you should say that 'cos he's the same here," she answered. "don't know why."

"What's going on, who is this?" rasped a voice from behind me.

I turned to see a thin, pale-faced man, with glassy eyes watching me, slouched up against the door frame and smoking. For the first time since starting this job I felt uncomfortable and wary. I was also beginning to realise why Marty was like he was. The sweet smell of 'waccy baccy' was thick in the air, and was starting to overwhelm me. I knew that I had to get out of the house and into the fresh air.

"She's from the school and wants to know why our Marty is always tired," said his wife.

"Now't wrong with him as far as I know," growled the man, menacingly.

Deciding it was time for me to go, I stood up.

"Well, if you think of anything will you please let us know?" I said. "I'll let myself out."

"Interfering busy body," I heard Mr Sinclair mutter.

My head was pounding by the time I reached the welcome fresh air outside, and my mouth was as dry as a bone. No wonder poor Marty struggled to motivate himself, living in an atmosphere like that. At least we now knew and understood why he was like he was, and could possibly take steps to help him.

I climbed into my car and breathed a sigh of relief. My eyes were itching and looked red. I wondered to myself how people got into such situations. It is very sad in a way, but what is even sadder is the effect that it has on their children. Even though I didn't like to think about it, there was a drug culture on the estate. Whether I liked it or not, I knew who the drug dealers were as did most of the people who live on the estate. Their respective wives were three of the most aggressive, unhappy individuals I knew.

For the first time ever I took myself home. I could smell the smoke on my clothes, so I had a shower, changed my clothes and got myself together for the afternoon.

CHAPTER 6

Greta's Revolt

The Parents' Room continued to be busy with close contacts being maintained with the local senior schools. Groups still went swimming every week in a school pool, whilst other groups made use of the badminton and squash courts. The netball team went from strength to strength and now belonged to a local league. Casey had completed sewing her wedding dress, and had now embarked on making the bridesmaid dresses for her two daughters.

The local football community team visited the school on a weekly basis, taking groups of children for ball skills activities. They came on a Thursday and joined in the lunchtime meal before the activities in the afternoon. There was a noticeable evidence of extra eye make-up and lipstick on these occasions.

Greta continued to be the main stalwart of the Room, and she and I had developed a special understanding and growing friendship. She was my eyes and ears when I was out of the Room, but always remained loyal to the group. However, she had no hesitation in telling them straight if she thought anyone overstepped the mark and let the Room down.

The one thing that really used to wind her up was people who sneaked out without washing their mugs.

One week she decided to make a stand. From Monday morning she only washed her own mug and put it away in the cupboard. By Wednesday morning, the sink was full of unwashed crockery and the supply of clean mugs was rapidly coming to an end. By Thursday morning, the only clean mug in the cupboard was Greta's. Carol wandered in, sat Chloe down on the floor, switched the kettle on and opened the cupboard door.

"Don't you dare touch that mug," yelled an irate Greta, who was right behind her.

"But there are no clean ones," exclaimed Carol.

"Why do you think that is?" questioned Greta, waving her ciggie in the air.

"'Cos you haven't washed them up," Carol replied, with that toothy uncertain grin.

I waited for the explosion.

"Why the bloody hell should I wash them up all the time?" Greta yelled, waving her ciggie again, with ash floating everywhere.

"I dunno," spluttered Carol, going red in the face.

Several more people had arrived by now and heard the commotion.

"Greta is quite right," said Emma, arriving at the sink. "Why should she clear up after us all of the time? Right, anyone who wants a drink can wash a mug for themselves."

Looking rather sheepish, one by one they took turns at the sink to clean a mug and make a drink.

Greta sat in the armchair with a mug in one hand, a ciggie in the other and a wry smile on her face. Later that day, Carol arrived in the Room with a splendid bouquet of flowers for Greta. The group had had a collection amongst themselves for the flowers and to say sorry to Greta for taking her for granted. I suspect that some of them could ill afford to contribute, but had done so, such is their own pride and respect for Greta. The washing up became less of an issue, and peace and harmony was restored – for a while.

The Easter holidays were approaching and Greta was in the throws of organising a coach trip to Skegness for a day. This was not just for the Parents' Room, as she was heavily involved with the Community Centre on the estate, and there would be at least three coaches going. I usually went on these days out, but I had a football match to attend so I was giving the outing a miss. The coaches were leaving from outside a shop on the estate, affectionately know as Shabby Syd's. I went down to wave them off, and as I watched them go, I realised with a jolt, that I knew every face at the windows on three fifty-seater coaches.

Waving to the happy, smiling expectant faces I felt a tug on my heartstrings. I was proud of some of their achievements and was becoming protective towards these lovely people. For many of them, this day out was the highlight of their year, and the only time they left the town. Every child would be given a lucky bag with a sugar laden drink and sweets which would send them 'hypo'. Name cards would be the order of the day to raise funds to thank the coach drivers and to buy their lunches. Greta always did the right thing.

CHAPTER 7

Nursery Life

The Easter holidays were over, and I was walking across the car park, contemplating what this term would bring. I could not believe that I had been in this job for nearly a year. As I approached the Room I could see someone hunched up sitting on the paving slabs, propped up against the wall. I began to feel a little apprehensive, wondering who it was and what was the matter. I slowed down to get a better look and to gather my thoughts. As I reached the gate, I could see some golden curls straying from the pulled up hood, and relief washed over me as I realised it was Casey; but what was she doing here so early? As she heard the sneck on the gate click open, she looked up and attempted a watery smile. Her face looked white and drawn, and her eyes looked puffy and dull.

"Casey, whatever is the matter?" I asked, worriedly.

Tears began to roll down her pale cheeks.

"Come on, let's get in and you can tell me what's going on," I said, unlocking the door.

Casey slumped down in a chair, and I wondered what had happened to this vibrant, lovely person in three weeks.

"It's been awful," she said, sniffing, "we have argued all the holiday, the poor kids have had a miserable time and it's all my fault."

"What caused the arguments?" I enquired.

"Can't you guess?" she answered.

"I probably can, but I want you to tell me," I replied.

"Booze! We have both been drinking far too much, and Sal, I think it's got to be a problem with me."

"Do you think you need help with it?" I asked gently, handing her a mug of coffee.

"Yes, I know I do," she answered, honestly, "Ian does but he won't admit it."

"Let's get you sorted out first, and then he might follow," I suggested. "I'll make some enquiries about getting some help for you, or do you want to do that?"

"I'll go to the doctors and see what he says. Thanks Sal, I just needed someone to talk to. It's a relief to share it with somebody," Casey replied.

"Let me know how it goes. Oh, here comes the mob – look out – normal service is resuming," I chuckled.

"You call this place normal?" Casey grinned, "it's good to be back."

I actually felt a pang of guilt that the Room had been shut for the holidays, and Casey had developed problems over that short space of time....but then, I needed time to recharge my batteries as well.

Greta appeared at the door with the familiar ciggie hanging from the corner of her mouth. Her weathered face crinkled into a warm smile.

"Hi everyone," she called.

"Hi Greta," came back the chorus.

"Did the day trip go well?" I enquired.

"Yes. Very good, except that I got there in my slippers and had to buy some flip-flops when we got to Skegness," Greta chuckled, waving a foot towards me with a bright pink flip-flop on it.

"Oh, very posh," I laughed.

"I threw the slippers away, they were knackered anyway," she grinned, "and then I needed some new slippers of course."

Sipping my coffee I glanced around the room. Casey had cheered up and was happily chatting to Emma, whose mop of black hair looked darker than ever. Carol and Janine were in deep conversation, whilst Abbey was sitting quietly by herself next to Cassie. Cassie's spiky, blond hair looked stiffer than usual, and her eye make-up looked very heavy – she was obviously trying to disguise a black eye. Perhaps her husband had caught her with her boyfriend and this was probably the consequence! I decided not to bring up the subject because I knew she would tell me if she wanted to – there was a lesson here for her to learn!

"No Sara today?" I questioned Casey.

"She'll be here in a minute," she replied. "She went into town with me last week for the first time in years. She was a trembling heap, but she did it."

"Wow, that's great!" I exclaimed, "Well done you."

"I haven't done anything," Casey replied.

"Yes you have," I answered, "your support has helped to give her the confidence to do that."

"Do you really think so?" she said, growing a little in stature.

I nodded and smiled. Much to my surprise Sara arrived on her own. I made a mental note to congratulate her on her achievement when the Room was quieter.

"There's a chair here, Sara," called the usually quiet Abbey.

Sara made herself a drink and sat down next to Abbey.

Even though she had made great strides since the netball match, Abbey had still not ventured in town. Sara's eyes were alive and shining as she described her trip into town.

"You'll have to come with us the next time we go. How about it?" she asked Abbey.

"I'll think about it," came the reply, a smile flittering across her face.

I marvelled at this Room. The support they gave each other was amazing, even though they didn't know it themselves.

Later that day, Casey came to tell me that she had seen her doctor who was going to make an appointment with Alcoholics Anonymous.

"I didn't have time to tell you this morning, but I got so desperate I rang the Samaritans," she confessed.

"It got that bad?" I asked, feeling for this young mother.

She nodded with tears threatening to fall again.

"Yeah. I spent all the money I had on booze, and had to borrow off Mum to feed the kids. How low can you get?" she choked.

"Look Casey, I agree that it's not good, but you have realised you need help and have done something about it, so feel proud of yourself for that," I said gently.

"I guess so," she answered with a bleak smile. "I'd better be off. Thanks Sal."

"Bye Casey, take care see you tomorrow."

I realised there was an awful amount of educating to be done to break this circle of unacceptable behaviour that was so normal to so many.

The Head Teacher, Mrs Harper, came across to the Room one Friday morning.

"Hi Sal," she said. "Sorry to do this, but the Nursery is a teacher short, and we can't get a supply in. Would you mind helping out?"

"Of course I'll help," I said, feeling rather panicky.

It had been a while since I had worked with the children – I hoped that I could remember what to do. I went to the Nursery and found that I was going to be in charge of one of the full-time groups. We had Circle Time, where the register was taken, and then a singing activity all about numbers, for about fifteen minutes. The children then went to their play area.

One little boy was playing with the floor road map, and was crashing cars together with as much force as he could. He had rosy, chubby cheeks and big, blue eyes.

"Be careful, Billy. You'll break those," I said, sitting next to him. "It's not a good idea."

"Well, this is what you do," came a grinning reply

"What do you mean?" I asked, "this is what you do."

"Well, when I get big, I am going to race cars round the green, and then set fire to them," he answered as if it was quite normal behaviour – he was four years old!

The thought struck me that it was normal behaviour for him at the time, as this was happening down his street on a regular basis. I tried to explain to him, that it was not the right thing to do, but clearly he was not convinced.

The Nursery was having a fun sports afternoon, and the children were very excited as their parents/carers were coming to watch. We had put out the small Nursery chairs for them to sit on.

As I walked out with my group, I bumped into Doreen with her usual foam, pink rollers dangling out from under her red and blue headscarf. She had come to watch her granddaughter.

"Where are we going to sit?" she enquired.

"On the chairs there," I replied, pointing to the small chairs.

"What? You expect me to get my fanny on that?" she spluttered, spray from her mouth going everywhere, and her rollers bobbing at an alarming rate.

Stepping back, I answered quickly.

"Well, if I can get my fanny on there, I'm sure you can."

Her mouth fell open in amazement, and it took me all my time not to explode with laughing. I really shouldn't have said that, I don't know where it came from. When I looked round, Doreen had sat down and was still staring at me in astonishment. For once she was speechless!

The following Monday, I was asked to help out again. It was just my luck that the OFSTED Inspectors were in school again for a lightning visit. It was the turn of the parents to be invited to Circle Time with the group of full-time children I was teaching. There were thirteen children in the group and nine parents had come to join in. The children were sitting on the floor with the parents sitting on benches behind them. As I began Circle Time, all about shapes, an Inspector clutching a clip board quietly joined the group. I concentrated on the children, but was very aware of the interloper in the group. The activities were going well and the children were responsive. I gradually relaxed and glanced up to see nine parents sitting bolt upright all with their arms folded, and concentration plastered over their faces. I swallowed and suppressed a chuckle – bless them, they were not going to let their children down. If the Inspector noticed he didn't say a word, except in his report where he wrote about the parents in glowing terms.

In the afternoon, I was in charge of the wet area with all the messy activities –water tray, sand and painting.

"What do you think of this then?" asked a squeaky, excitable voice.

I looked up from the sand tray to see a vision in gold standing before me.

"Debbie, what are you doing with that on in here?" I spluttered. "be careful of those paint brushes."

Debbie was a relatively new comer to the Parents' Room. She was a sweet lady who sometimes lived in a simple, but not quite real, world. She had a daughter who had special needs that Debbie found difficult to understand and accept.

"It's my new, gold ball gown. Do you like it?" she beamed, twirling round. "I just thought that you would like to see it."

Its full skirt was brushing dangerously close to the red paint pot.

"It's lovely. What ball are you going to?" I enquired.

"I'm not. I bought it in case a handsome man takes me to one," she explained, peering through her pink-framed glasses.

"I don't think you ought to be in here with it on. It could get ruined with some paint," I said, and what would the Inspector think if he returned.

"No, the children wouldn't mess it up," she answered. "What do you think children?"

At this she flung her arms wide and pirouetted around the sand tray. The children didn't bat an eyelid, as if this happened every day in the Nursery.

"Debbie," I exclaimed sharply, "back to the Parents' Room please."

"Okay. See you," she sang as she danced her way through the Nursery.

The next day the Nursery was fully staffed and I was able to return to the Room and keep its occupants in check.

Parents were encouraged to come and help out in school, and could be found in most classrooms. Their help was greatly valued and, in time, many of them grew in confidence and self-worth. Some of them came into the Parents' Room but not all of them – it was not everyone's cup of tea. It was part of my job to visit some families who had a child that would be eligible to have a part-time Nursery place. The purpose was to arrange a time for their child to look round the Nursery and to meet their teacher.

"We'll send you to visit Mrs Sykes," said Laura, who was in charge of Nursery admissions.

"Why are you grinning like that?" I asked nervously.

The rest of the staff sitting round the table chuckled.

"You'll find out. She only wants to take up a full-time place," replied Laura.

"Come on, give me some info so that I know what to expect," I pleaded.

"For some reason, Mrs Sykes doesn't like sending her children to part-time Nursery, and she can get rather cross when offered one, although she always fills in the forms. I must admit she scares me," Laura confessed.

"Oh, thanks for that. I'll tread carefully!" I replied. "I'll go tomorrow and get it over with."

"We'll come and look for you if you are not back by dinner time," Laura offered, smiling.

The next day I decided to walk on my Nursery visits as they were all near to the school, and I thought that the fresh air would clear my lungs. I think the smoke extractor in the Room needs urgent attention.

The first house I came to on my list, was a neatly kept property with a bright red front door. I was just about to knock on it when it suddenly flew open, and I was greeted by a fresh faced, heavily pregnant young woman.

"Hi, I saw you coming. I hope you've come to offer Ebony a place," she said cheerily.

"Quite right, Mrs Lee, I have," I said smiling.

"Come in. Do you fancy a cuppa?" she asked.

I decided to decline the offer based on past experiences, but I am sure it would have been fine in this clean, neatly kept house.

"I can see why you called her Ebony," I commented as a pretty young girl with a mass of jet-black curls appeared.

"She is so ready for Nursery," Mrs Lee chattered, "and it will be easier for me when the baby comes. I'm fair bursting. Jack! The teacher is here from school."

Jack joined us. He was a tall, good looking young man, who also had a mop of black curly hair. As I was explaining about the Nursery, I was aware that Jack was scrutinising me very closely.

"Now, is there anything you want to ask me?" I enquired.

"Yes. Were you at the football match on Saturday," Jack asked, "in the Pontoon?"

"Jack! She didn't mean about that," Mrs Lee scolded. "Sorry."

"It's okay, yes I was there. It wasn't very good at all was it?" I replied.

"No, there was more ball control in the men's loo at half-time than there was on the pitch," Jack proclaimed with passion.

"Jack, don't talk like that. I'm sorry," spluttered Mrs Lee, going red in the face.

"Don't worry, I hear much worse than that at the matches," I laughed. "On that note I really must be on my way. You'll be hearing from school shortly."

Chuckling my way down the path, I realised that Mrs Sykes was next on my list.

Ah well – into battle.

A few doors down and what a contrast. The gate was hanging off its hinges, and a drive full of litter greeted me. I knocked on the shabby, yellow front door and waited with bated breath. The door opened a crack.

"What is it?" growled a voice.

"I'm from the Nursery Mrs Sykes. I've come to offer you a part-time morning place for Tommy."

The door opened to reveal a large lady dressed in a baggy black T-shirt and black leggings.

"Not seen you before. Who are you? What's your name?" she demanded.

"I'm Sally Brown and I work in the Parents' Room, but I also help out the Nursery with visits," I answered as calmly as I could.

"I've heard about that Room. Not very good things though," she retorted, glaring at me as if I was on a recruiting drive

"I'm not here to talk about the Parents' Room Mrs Sykes. I've come to talk about Tommy and the Nursery," I replied, smiling as best as I could.

She looked at me as if I should not be smiling, and for a fleeting moment I saw warmth in those big, brown eyes glowering at me. She actually had a beautifully sculptured face, framed by long, thick, brown hair – if only she would smile and not frown.

Three year old Tommy arrived at the door. He had a mop of tousled brown curls and startling blue eyes. He immediately threw his arms around his mum's leg and clung on. Mrs Sykes picked him up and a transformation took place. Her whole demeanour softened when she looked at her cheeky-faced son. He gurgled with delight as he grabbed hands full of her hair, and she smiled with sheer delight.

"He's a lovely boy," I ventured, "he would love Nursery."

Her face darkened again, and I thought that I had gone too far.

"Do you know why I am not keen on him coming to Nursery?" she enquired.

"No I don't, but I should like you to tell me," I replied.

A ghost of a smile played on her lips.

"You're the first one to ask. The others used to dash away from me like a rabbit caught in headlights," she exclaimed. "I thought well, if they can't be bothered to ask, I'm not telling them."

"Okay, I'm listening with all ears," I encouraged her.

"Well, I'm not one of those mums who can't wait to get their kids out of their hair. I enjoy my children, and love doing things with them. I play games with them, and tell them stories and all that," she explained.

"I think that's wonderful," I answered. "You must be a great mum."

"You do?" she answered, looking at me in astonishment.

"Yes, I do, but you could have the best of both worlds you know," I explained. "If Tommy came to Nursery in the morning, you could come and help, and then he would be mixing with the other children, but you would be there as well."

The glimmer of a smile was there again.

"Think about it," I said, "there's no pressure on you. When you decide, come and see me, but don't leave it too long."

She thought for a moment.

"Okay," she nodded, "but I'm not coming in that Room."

"No, you don't have to. I'm always somewhere down the corridor in the morning. Cheerio now, see you soon I hope," I called, as I picked my way through the rubbish on the drive.

"Thank you for listening," a voice called.

I turned round and waved.

I completed all my home visits with a spring in my step, and returned to school.

"How did you get on with Mrs Sykes?" asked Laura as soon as I popped into the Nursery.

"She is going to let me know," I replied quietly.

"Didn't think you would get anywhere, we never do." came the answer. "All she does is complain."

The next morning I was in the Room and the door partly opened – it was Mrs Sykes.

"Can I have a word?" she called from the Nursery cloakroom.

"Hi, nice to see you," I smiled.

"I want Tommy to have his morning Nursery place, and I should like to help too ...please," she said, almost smiling.

"That's great. I'll let the staff know," I enthused. "See you when he comes for his visit."

"That's tomorrow, see you then," she replied and was gone.

"What did she want? Complaining again?" asked Laura.

"No, she wants Tommy to have his morning place, and she would like to come to help in the Nursery," I replied, trying not to sound too smug.

The ashen look on Laura's face was all I needed.

Every so often, I went into the school assemblies, and people from the Room took it in turns to accompany me. They loved joining in the singing, and they took part in the sunflower growing competition. Our sunflower was planted outside in the Room's garden, and was ferociously guarded by Carol and Greta as it flourished and grew. Whoa betide anyone who touched it.

Janine was in charge of watering it and she always took her son Adam and some of the other youngsters to help her out. Every so often she would measure it and keep a record on a chart. She rightly thought that if she taught the youngsters how to look after it themselves, they would not damage it. I hoped and prayed that no-one would come along after school and destroy it.

CHAPTER 8
Carnival Time

There was great excitement when the local newspaper rang to see if they could do an article about the Parents' Room and take photographs. The amount of make-up on the faces was amazing - I thought that they had all got jobs as fashion models overnight.

The reporter and photographer came and were made very welcome. As I listened to their replies to the questions asked, I realised how far some of them had come and how much their self-esteem had grown. They were actually proud of themselves at last. They all had lovely smiles on their faces as the photographer took a group picture and then some of them cooking. They were highly delighted when the reporter and photographer accepted an invitation to stop and have shepherd's pie for lunch. They were both amazed that such a delicious meal could be cooked for so many on a Baby Belling cooker. A few days later the article was in the paper, and what a super report it was. It was a wonder that the Gazette didn't sell out – everyone had more than one copy to send to family and friends.

There were six weeks to go before the end of term, and Casey's wedding was fast approaching. It was going to be on the first Saturday of the holiday. She had just about finished the final touches to the bridesmaid dresses for her daughters when she came up with a crazy idea!

"Sal," she said, "we've all been talking and we'd love to have a float in the town carnival. Will you help us to organise it?"

"When is it?" I asked hesitantly.

"Eerr, Friday evening, the day before my wedding," Casey spluttered.

"You've got to be joking," I gasped. "it's too much to organise."

"Oh please," came a chorus of expectant voices. "we'll all help."

"I've heard that one before," chortled Greta, puffing away. "Anyway, who's going to winch me up onto a lorry?"

"And where am I going to get a lorry from at this short notice?" I asked, but I already thought I could, because a good friend of mine owned a haulage company.

"Come on Sal, it will be good fun....please," begged Emma, tossing her mane of black hair over her shoulders. "We've never done anything like it before in our lives."

"How many of you are up for it?" I asked nervously.

"Me, me, me," came the eager chorus

"I really don't know," I replied, thoughts whirling round in my head.

"We should like to do it too," came a quiet voice.

I looked to see who it was and realised that I had lost the argument in that moment. It was Sara and Abbey sitting together, smiling at me. They were both making such an effort to overcome their fear of going out into the wide world. How could I refuse now?

"Okay, okay, you win, but you must all promise to help me and we pull together. No bickering or falling out over things," I sighed, giving in gracefully.

They clapped and chattered excitedly at the thought of what was to come.

"Just one thing though, what is the theme of the float?" I enquired.

"Disney characters," they all replied at once, laughing.

"Oh I see. You've got all this sussed out already," I chuckled, "there will be a lot to do making costumes."

"Well, Casey has finished all her wedding dresses, so we thought we could make them in sewing classes with Jane," answered Abbey grinning, "she doesn't mind."

"Well, you are organised aren't you, you crafty monkeys," I smiled, looking at their happy faces. "Okay, I'll try to get the lorry and scaffolding sorted out tonight. I think I know someone who will help. Now come on, haven't you got homes to go to?

"Mugs!" shouted Greta, "I can see you sneaking out."

Mugs were washed and put away, and they went off talking noisily, walking down the school path.

Only Greta was left and I groaned wearily to her, "What have we let ourselves in for? What character have you got me down for?"

"Dumbo," chortled Greta, "night love, sleep tight, see you tomorrow?"

After rather frantic negotiations I managed to secure a lorry and scaffolding courtesy of my friend Joe, and the use of a generator from another firm in town.

The last week of the summer term arrived all too soon. All of the sunflowers were measured and the Parents'

Room came a creditable third – somehow the plant had survived. Parents' evenings were over – some were happier than others. The children knew whose class they would be going into next school term – again some were happier than others. Much to their and our delight, Jill Sykes and Janine announced that they had enrolled onto a Child Development course in September – wonderful.

I helped Casey to transport her wedding dresses to her mum's house for safe keeping.

Excitement was growing as the carnival parade, and the wedding, drew near. Vibrant Disney character costumes festooned the Room waiting for their finishing touches in the sewing class this week. Mrs Harper had invited them to go into the end of term assembly and show the children their costumes. Scenes from Disney films were being stored in the school boiler room, painted on large boards of plywood. These props were ready to be fastened onto the scaffolding on the lorry. It was Abbey's idea to draw and paint the boards.

"I was quite good at drawing and art when I was at school," she suddenly announced. She encouraged Sara to help her and the finished products were quite amazing. The paintings of the seven dwarfs were a delight to look at and brought a smile to everyone's faces when they saw them. Other painted characters included Dumbo, Peter Pan and Captain Hook along with scenes from the Lion King. As praise was heaped on her, I am sure Abbey grew by two inches. Sara also visibly grew in confidence. These two ladies were becoming very good friends and they were helping each other to overcome their shyness amongst other problems. The days when Abbey hid behind her long hair, were now very few and far between.

The Room was buzzing as they donned their costumes to parade before the children at the final school year assembly. The children and staff gathered expectantly in the hall. With Mrs Harper playing the piano they sang the lively hymn 'The Lord of the Dance' with great enthusiasm. Scrambling quickly into my Evil Queen costume borrowed from Greta, we all gathered in the cloakroom to make our entrance into the hall.

"Now children, we have a special treat," I heard Mrs Harper say, "some of our lovely parents are taking part in the carnival parade in town next week, and have come to show us the beautiful costumes that they have made. Let's see if we can guess who they are supposed to be."

A ripple of excitement went round the hall.

"You go first Greta," I said. She was resplendent as Cruella de Vil from a Hundred and One Dalmatians. Her black and white wig was back-combed to its limit. A black and white dotted cape over a black dress, red shoes and gloves completed the stylish outfit perfectly.

The children clapped and guessed the characters as they entered the hall, one by one. Abbey was Mickey Mouse, closely followed by Sara, who was Minnie Mouse. Emma, looking vibrant with her abundant long black hair, was Pocahontas. Our athletic Lizzie was dressed in green and flew in as Peter Pan, with Pete chasing her as Captain Hook. Chris, who was recovering from breast cancer, bravely danced in as Tinkerbell. Janine was colourful as Winnie the Pooh, and she was followed by Carol as Donald Duck who proceeded to quack as loudly as she could. Andy pirouetted, brightly dressed as Pinocchio, with a false nose on. Casey as Snow White and I as the Wicked Queen brought the final line up.

Mrs Harper went along the line of characters saying a few words to each one. As she arrived at Andy he reached under his hat and suddenly his false nose shot out in front of him, making poor Mrs Harper jump out of her skin. Greta looked aghast.

"Andy!" she hissed, "stop it now."

Andy reached under his hat but the nose kept growing.

"I can't, it won't stop," he spluttered. The children started to giggle, and I could see Mrs Harper trying not to laugh. As I glanced around, I could see some of the staff grinning, whilst the usual one or two looked on with total distain.

"Andy, just wave and go," I whispered quietly, trying frantically to keep a straight face. He took the hint and quickly disappeared, taking his ever growing nose with him.

Mrs Harper recovered herself sufficiently to announce that the children would sing one more song while the rest of the characters left the hall.

"Whatever do you think you were frigging well playing at?" cried Greta as she came bursting through the Room door, jabbing her red gloved fingers in her son's direction, and her black and white wig wobbling vigorously on her head.

"I was getting into character", replied Andy, innocently. "Pinocchio's nose grew every time he told a lie."

"Well, you've really embarrassed me. Fancy wearing an inflatable nose in front of the children, never mind the teachers," grumbled Greta, glaring at Andy and throwing her wig on the table, as she reached for a ciggie.

"Where did you get that nose from?" enquired Carol sitting next to Andy.

Janine suddenly chuckled.

"What's so funny?" growled Greta, puffing away.

"I don't think it's a nose," giggled Janine, "have a look".

Casey and Carol came to inspect 'the nose'

"It's a willy," cried Carol dressed as Donald Duck, "quack, quack, go on Andy, give us a blast".

Andy reached up under his hat and the nose began to grow.

"It's an inflatable willy!" cried Abbey, laughing loudly. "I'll see if my Jack wants one."

This was an unprecedented outburst from Abbey who clapped her hand across her mouth when she realised what she had said. The room dissolved into laughter.

"Perhaps we could order a job lot," chortled Emma loudly.

"What's up Greta, you alright?" asked Pete amongst the hilarity.

All eyes rested upon Greta. She was sitting at the table with her hands covering her weather worn face and shoulders shaking.

"Oh Greta, don't get upset. Nobody else realised what it was," said Sara, giving the older lady a warm hug.

Greta's shoulders shook even more, and tears appeared to trickle under her hands.

"Where are the tissues? She's crying now," declared Carol, "here you are," she continued, pushing a tissue into Greta's cupped hand.

A muffled spluttering sound came from the bereft lady as she took her hands away from her face.

"I'm laughing you twits," she cried, taking off her glasses and wiping her eyes.

"Did you see the look on that stuck-up Mrs Amble's face? It was priceless. That'll teach her to look down her nose at us."

"I'll pretend I didn't hear that," I said, smiling secretly in agreement. "Right, we've had a good laugh and, like you said Sara, I don't think anyone else noticed."

With decorum and order safely restored the end of term arrived.

"Cheers everybody, see you on Friday at St Peter's Park for the parade, and don't be late, please," I implored.

With children collected from various classrooms, the parents disappeared down the school path across the field, clutching their precious costumes. I sat down to enjoy the rare silence of the Room as the elegant Mrs Harper appeared through the door. She flung herself into the old easy chair in the corner and kicked her shoes off. If only the parents could have seen her!

"Oh Sal, that was quite a memorable assembly," she remarked, seriously.

"Err yes, sorry about that," I replied, meekly.

A mischievous smile flickered across Mrs Harper's face and her bright eyes sparkled with amusement.

"If that was an inflatable nose, I'll eat my hat," she quipped, roaring with laughter. "Enjoy the hols."

CHAPTER 9
Carnival Day

The day of the carnival arrived and I woke up with some trepidation. I had never attempted anything like this before, and I suppose I was worried they would not turn up, as it had been a few days since I had seen any of the group since the holidays had begun. I collected the generator that had been so generously loaned for free, and made my way to meet the lorry at the assembly point in the Park.

"Hi Sal," Joe called cheerily from the cab of the lorry, "are you ready for this?"

"I really don't know. I must admit I am nervous," I replied. "I just hope that they turn up."

"I don't think you need to worry about that," grinned Joe, looking over my shoulder.

Turning round, I didn't know whether to laugh or cry with relief. Walking towards me was a glittering Disney fairytale castle, at least seven feet high! As the vision drew closer, I could see four pairs of feet walking with it and then out popped Abbey's face.

"Yoo hoo Sal, what do you think, do you like it?" she shouted when in hearing range.

"It's fabulous, looks great," I called back, "so good to see you Abbey"

"I'm here too," chirped another voice.

It was Sara. Who would have believed it? Sara and Abbey walking through the park, carrying a fairytale castle – six months ago that would have been unheard of. The other four feet belonged to Casey and Lizzie and they were red faced, giggling and out of breath. They propped the castle up against the lorry.

"Phew, that took some doing, I need a fag," gasped Casey.

"Where have you carried it from?" I enquired.

"My house," replied Abbey,

"You've carried this all the way from the Meadows?" I asked incredulously, "how long has it taken you?"

"Only about forty five minutes. It's only made of strong cardboard, so I hope it doesn't rain or get too windy. We decided that we needed something to make an impact on the lorry. We've been making it since the kids broke up," explained Abbey.

"Very impressive," exclaimed Joe looking on in admiration. "You've worked very hard, it looks quite sturdy."

Looking at their excited faces, how could I have doubted that they would turn up? What was I thinking of?

"Pete is bringing the rest of the props, and our costumes, in his van, but this was too big to fit in it. The rest of them are on their way," continued Lizzie, doing a few stretching exercises.

"Good God Lizzie, haven't you just done enough exercising?" exclaimed Casey, laughing. "I'm knackered."

"You can never do enough exercising," replied Lizzie "keeps you feeling young."

Pete arrived and unloaded the brightly painted Disney props to cover the scaffolding on the lorry.

He helped Joe to load the generator onto the lorry, and then dropped the costumes off at Melanie's house. Melanie was a worker in the mobile crèche at school. Her house was opposite the Park and she offered us the use of it to change into our costumes, (brave lady).

Pete parked his van outside Melanie's terraced house and came back to help decorate the lorry. The rest of the gang had arrived and were enthusiastically helping each other. Greta was directing operations from a camping chair, making encouraging noises in between ciggies. Perhaps most important of all, they were having fun, and it was a delight to observe. The generator was up and running, and music and songs from Disney films rang out from large speakers.

The Park was full of lorries being trimmed and decorated for the parade, and everyone was sportingly helping each other out with tape, blue tack and string. Laughter resounded round the Park, and the occasional 'bloody hell' or words to that effect could be heard when a balloon burst making everybody jump.

All too soon it was time to dash across the Park and descend on Melanie's house to get changed into our costumes ready for the big parade. We had made it though – the lorry was decorated (and I know that I am biased) but it looked magnificent. Melanie had laid on tea and sandwiches which was a lovely surprise, and very kind of her. Her little house was soon immersed in clouds of hair spray, Mickey Mouse ears, Indian head dresses, fairy wings, and Carol quacking. Melanie didn't mind one bit, saying that she was enjoying sharing the experience. Really!!??

Clutching carrier bags with our everyday clothes inside, we trooped back to the lorry.

"You all look great," Joe greeted us. "Let's get you all onto the lorry – we go in fifteen minutes."

Thoughtfully, Joe had brought a small set of steps to help everyone to get on board as elegantly as possible. He took photographs to capture the event for posterity, and then climbed into his cab ready to go.

Out of eighty floats we were number thirty. The stewards expertly guided the lorries out of the narrow park gateway, and Joe started the engine as it was nearly our turn to go. I looked round at the expectant faces, and realised that nervous expressions were evident.

"Don't look so worried, we look super, so just relax and enjoy the experience," I called. Look out for your families and friends on route."

The Bare Necessities from Jungle Book boomed out of the speakers, and Greta began to sing at the top her voice, clicking her fingers to the beat. Carol joined in with the occasional quack as she sang, which made everyone laugh and soon they were all singing along. They visibly relaxed as we emerged into the street and saw the crowds lining the pavements waving at them.

Every so often they saw members of their family and the cheering became louder as they frantically waved their arms.

The band played as the parade made its way slowly along the route. I noticed that Carol was wiping her eyes and smudging her make-up.

"Are you crying"? I asked as quietly as I could in the midst of the noise.

"Yes," she sniffed.

"Why? What is it?" I asked, rather concerned.

"I didn't think anyone would come and see me, 'cos mum is in a wheel chair and she said she couldn't come, but we've just passed her, and Tommy, her next door neighbour. He must have brought her and she had Chloe on her knee."

"That's brill," I replied. "so dry those tears and enjoy the rest of the parade."

"Do you know, Sal, she looked so proud of me? I could tell, she's never looked at me like that before," she revealed.

All I could do was to give her a hug and feel happy for her.

"Go on Pinocchio, grow that nose" I heard Casey shout.

The others shrieked with laughter as Pinocchio reached under his hat and his nose began to grow!

The parade came to an end, and we finished the amazing evening off at the carnival disco, which was great fun. I refrained from staying too late as it was Casey's wedding the next day.

I hoped that she didn't get too carried away with the carnival atmosphere and have too much to drink – she was progressing so well. As I bid her goodnight I was tempted to say something to her, but no – I had to have faith in her.

CHAPTER 10

Wedding Nerves

I was up at the crack of dawn the next morning. My car needed cleaning inside and out as I was chauffeur for the wedding day, and also photographer. The Adult Education Centre had loaned us a camera so that I could record the wedding. I battled with very slippery, satin wedding ribbon trying to decorate the car. I suddenly became so tired I felt like having a good cry but decided I didn't have time. After a quick shower, I put on my cream and brown striped suit trying to look like a chauffeur and also photographer. Making sure I had all that I needed, I set off to collect Casey and her two girls to go to the Register Office for the morning ceremony. As I pulled up outside her house I could see two little faces peering out of the window and waving.

The front door flew open as I walked down the path, and all my fears from the previous evening disappeared as a radiant Casey stood in the doorway. The creamy lace dress emphasised her slimline figure, and a silk head dress of small pale peach roses hugged her mass of tumbling golden curls that framed her delightful, fresh smiling face.

"You look beautiful," I exclaimed, hugging her gently. Some people would frown upon such a show of affection from a member of staff, but that was my way, and the only way I knew, of how to do the job.

"Thanks Sal," she replied, tears glinting in her eyes. "Come on in, Mum is here trying to keep the girls clean."

Casey's two little daughters, Eva and Sophie, were in the lounge with their grandma Joyce. Casey had had no contact with her father for years.

"You look a picture," I smiled as the girls beamed proudly back at me.

"Come on, let's take some pictures before we go," I exclaimed.

I took various photos of them individually, in pairs and the three female generations of the family. Casey had a bouquet of deep peach roses and the girls had matching posy baskets.

A taxi pipped outside, ready to take Joyce to the Register Office. She hugged her daughter and two granddaughters, and hurried out to the waiting car, dabbing her eyes as she walked down the path.

"Right, are we ready?" I enquired.

"We're ready," replied Casey, "come on girls, let's go and meet Daddy and have a party."

"Yea!" clapped the girls. "We can show Daddy our new dresses," cried Eva.

"Hope he's not hung over from last night - he stayed at a mate's house," whispered Casey, as we got in the car. "You know what he can be like, not much will-power."

"Fingers crossed, we'll soon know," I answered optimistically. "I've just got to call and drop off the generator we used yesterday – it's on our way to the Register Office."

Casey chuckled, "This must be a first – the bride dropping off a generator on her way to her wedding."

We drove into the yard and parked near to the office. I got out of the car and opened the boot, while a young man appeared to help unload the machine. He peered into the car and saw Casey and the girls.

"Good grief, what's this? Are you off to a wedding?" he exclaimed, looking astonished."

"You could say that," I replied, laughing.

"Dad, dad, come here and look at this lot," the young man shouted, "Quick."

The office door flew open and an older man walked briskly to the car. His face broke into a smile when he saw the occupants.

"Go and fetch the others," he told the young man.

Five other people hurried from the office and peeped into the car. There were lots of 'ooos', and 'awhs', and 'how lovely'.

Casey treated them to a stunning smile and the girls giggled, enjoying all the attention. Two men unloaded the generator, repeated their good wishes and closed the car boot. As we drove out of the yard, the well-wishers clapped and waved us goodbye. Casey did an excellent version of 'the Royal wave' in return.

"Oh that was fun," she chortled, "did you see their faces?"

"I think you will be the talking point for quite some time," I laughed. "Right, let's get to the Register Office for the next part of the adventure."

I left Casey and the girls in the foyer, and went to join the other guests inside.

"There's a seat for you here," said Greta, looking very smart in a midnight blue suit and sparkling shoes to match.

"Many thanks," I replied. "There's a lot here. I like your shoes."

Looking round, I could see many of the gang from the Parents' Room dressed up to the nines in their best clothes - they had done us proud. Casey and Ian both had large families who were here in force, wearing anything from ripped jeans to smart jeans and smart suits.

"Where's Carol?" I asked.

"She's just nipped out the back for a fag," explained Greta, shrugging her shoulders. "Trust her not to be able to wait a few minutes. I thought that you were recording this."

"I am, but not until we get to the reception. They weren't keen on me filming in here," I answered. "How's Ian?"

"Looks very rough," whispered Greta.

"Oh no, Casey was really hoping he wouldn't have too much to drink last night," I groaned, my heart sinking.

"Look at Joyce's face," said Greta quietly. "She's furious."

Joyce was sitting bolt upright, with a face like thunder. Ian was sitting hunched over with his back to me so I could not see what state he was in. The door clattered open and Carol appeared with a bright red feathery fascinator perched on her light brown straggly hair do.

"It's bloody windy out there," she exclaimed as she made her way to her seat next to me. "Nearly blew my facilitator off,"

"It's a fascinator," I chuckled.

"Well, whatever it is," she cackled sitting down. "Ian looks pissed. Casey will go mad."

"Sshh stupid, don't let everyone know," hissed Greta, making even more noise. Joyce glanced round and glowered in our direction.

Elvis's 'Can't Help Falling in Love' began to play softly, the door opened and everyone stood up. Casey glided down the aisle smiling radiantly, followed by her two beautiful daughters. Joyce's thunderous expression softened a little as she saw them walking towards her. As Casey drew level with Ian her expression changed, and disappointment washed over her face for all to see. Her whole body stiffened and she stared stonily into Ian's bleary eyes.

"I'm so sorry," he whispered audibly, "really I am."

"Just for once I thought that you may behave yourself, I really did," Casey barked back, her voice breaking into a sob. "Why do you always let me down?"

"Is there a problem?" enquired the Registrar quietly.

"Please Casey, you know what I'm like and you all look so, so beautiful," Ian choked looking at Casey, and then at his two lovely girls, who were staring so trustingly at him. Everyone began to look uneasily at each other and shuffle backwards and forwards. Then the unthinkable happened – Ian broke into uncontrollable sobs. His shoulders trembled as he tried to regain his composure.

"Daddy, don't cry. Mummy, please make him stop. Daddy never cries," begged Sophie, pulling at Casey's dress, and waving her posy frantically. The expression on Casey's face softened, and her eyes glistened with tears that threatened to roll down her beautifully made-up face.

Placing her bouquet carefully on the Registrar's table, she turned and cupped Ian's face in her hands, brushed his tears away and gently kissed him on the cheek. She tenderly smiled at him through her tears and nodded her head. The silence in the room was deafening!

"Err, are we ready to continue?" asked the Registrar.

"Yes, as ready as we shall ever be," answered Casey, picking up her flowers. "Let's do this."

The girls beamed and there was a collective sigh of relief. Even Joyce looked more relaxed, and Ian pulled himself together and shot a watery, grateful smile at his beaming bride to be.

"Bloody hell! That was a close call. I thought for a minute I was going to miss out on the bun fight," hissed Carol. "I didn't have any breakfast and I'm starving."

"Trust you to think of your stomach - sshh, they are starting the ceremony," whispered Greta. The ceremony went off without further incident, and after the photographs we all adjourned to the Cherry Tree pub for the reception. I threw myself into official camera person mode, and generally made a nuisance of myself until the batteries ran out. Carol was first in line when the buffet opened, her red fluffy fascinator sliding further down her straw-like hair. Her plate was generously laden with a precariously balanced Scotch egg perched on top. With glass in one hand and the plate in the other, she manoeuvred around chairs and children. As she reached her table her balance deserted her, and the Scotch egg took off from her plate and rolled across the floor, much to the delight of the pursuing children.

"Oi, you little gits, that's mine," Carol yelled.

Too late! One well aimed, right footed kick and the egg became scrambled all over the small dance floor. A member of staff appeared from behind the bar with a dustpan and brush and disapproving glares.

"Who's that bloke Carol is sat with?" I asked Greta.

"I don't know, I've never seen him before," replied Greta. "Do any of you lot know?" she asked the others at our table. We were sitting with Sara, Janine, Emma, Lizzie and Abbey.

"It's Ben. He's Ian's cousin I think," answered Abbey, "a bit of a lad so I've heard."

"Carol is looking rather gooey eyed at him," commented Emma, "Don't know why though."

"Must be the beer," chuckled Greta, "this could spell trouble. Christ, these shoes are killing me."

With that she delved into her bottomless trademark bag, and fished out her pink flip-flops.

"Oh the relief," she grinned, wriggling her toes as she took off her posh shiny shoes and replaced them with her flip-flops. "Right, time for a fag!"

Gradually the reception drew to a close, as guests began to head for home, some steadier than others but all in good humour. Casey flopped down on the chair next to me.

"It's been a super do," I commented.

"Yeah, no fights, thank God," replied Casey, chuckling, "even Ian has behaved himself."

"You were very dignified at the Register Office," I said, "did you really have second thoughts?"

"Only for a moment," sighed Casey, "it really shocked me when he cried. I have never, ever seen him cry before, not even when the girls were born. I know what he is about and what he comes with, and I have my faults too that he puts up with....and I love him. We'll be alright if we work through things together."

"You'll be fine I'm sure. Just remember to always keep talking. Never bottle things up inside, that's when problems begin," I commented.

"Yes, Mum," chuckled Casey.

"Oh blimey, sorry, I'm preaching, I'll shut up and say my goodbyes," I laughed, hugging a very tired looking bride, and I began the long summer holiday.

CHAPTER 11

Courage and Flour

It seemed like in no time at all that I am parking my car in the school car park, ready for the Autumn Term. I wondered how they had all got on over the holiday without the support of the Parents' Room and each other. There had been some talk of meeting up on a regular basis at each other's houses, but I didn't know if they had actually organised anything.

"Kettle's on," called out a soft Scottish twang.

"Hi Greta, you are early," I replied, going into the very familiar cosy room with its battered looking, even scruffy, comfy chairs and settees. Making a mental note that I ought to do something about them, I smiled at Greta, who was sitting in state, with a mug of coffee and the ever present ciggie.

"Thought I would have a few quiet minutes before they all arrive. Have you had a good holiday?" she asked.

"Yes, great thanks. Had a week in the Lake District, and for once the weather was good," I said.

"I had a few days out. We went to Skeggy and Mablethorpe which were good. I won a set of pans at the bingo," explained Greta.

"Sounds like fun," I answered, "have you seen any of the others, are they alright?" I enquired.

"I've just seen them out and about on the estate. I think they are all okay. Carol has a new bloke in tow – it's that Ben chap she met at Casey's wedding," volunteered Greta.

"Oh my goodness, I guess we'll be hearing all about it soon," I chuckled.

"I hope she is being careful, or we shall be having another mini Carol on the way," smiled Greta, "don't know if we can cope with that...Oh look out, here they come."

First to clatter through the door was Casey with Sophie and Eva in tow.

"Hi Sal, it's great to be back, nice to see you as well," chattered Casey. "I've brought the wedding photos to show you. You did a great job."

"That's a relief," I replied, "I did wonder if they would turn out okay. I'll have a look at them later, here's a coffee."

"Thanks, I like this personal drinks service," she grinned.

"Cheeky, make the most of it, it won't happen again," I replied."

"Hello Sal, have you missed me?" called Carol, as she breezed through the door with Chloe.

"Yeah, like she misses toothache," laughed Casey.

I realised that I had missed this funny unique group of people. Gradually they arrived – Sara, Janine, Abbey, Lizzie, Pete, Chris and a few others soon filled the room with happy chatter. While we were all gathered together, I asked them what visits or talks they would like to have in the Room. We already had on - going English, Maths and sewing classes, which were always very well attended.

"What's in your mug?" asked Carol, hovering nearby.

"Tea, why?" I replied.

"Good, Chloe likes tea," and with that she dunked Chloe's dummy in my tea, and then plugged it in the little girl's mouth.

"You cheeky mare," exclaimed Greta aghast, "make your own tea."

"Welcome back Carol, nice to share things with you again," I chuckled, "you can make me a fresh cuppa now."

Carol just grinned and filled the kettle up.

As they all began to drift off, Lizzie remained behind. Greta was the last to leave to go and collect the prizes for the bingo that afternoon.

"Are you okay Lizzie?" I asked, as she usually departed with the others. She shifted uncomfortably in her chair and looked embarrassed. I sat next to her and waited.

"Can you tell me what it is?" I encouraged her.

Tears welled up in her eyes.

"I'm so embarrassed and ashamed," she replied.

"Go on, it can't be that bad, surely" I said quietly.

"Well, would you believe it that I can't read or write?" she sobbed. "I always struggled at school, and no-one seemed to have the time to help me, and I just muddled through."

"Oh Lizzie, it's nothing to be ashamed of. Please don't be so upset, we can help you. You can join the English classes here," I suggested.

"No, no I can't. I don't want anyone here to know," Lizzie cried, "but please can you help me? I just want to be like everyone else."

My mind went into overtime. What could I do to help Lizzie if she wouldn't join in the class here? I must say that I was rather amazed that a bright, energetic young lady like Lizzie was in this position. Still she had had the courage to reach out and ask for help – not an easy thing to do.

"Leave it with me and I'll make some enquiries and see what we can do. Don't worry, I'll be discreet."

"Thanks, Sal, that'll be great," she replied, with a watery smile. "Only my mum knows, but she is not bothered, as she can't read or write either, and she can't understand why I want to learn."

My heart went out to Lizzie – another person caught up in a fixed circle of life that hadn't been broken – but here she was asking for help to break it, and move into a whole new world of life changing experiences.

"I'll get back to you as soon as I can," I said.

"Okay, I'd better go and catch up with the others. They'll wonder what I've been doing," replied Lizzie.

"Bye Lizzie," I called as she disappeared through the door. I knew that I had to act quickly as it was the start of a new term and classes would be starting soon. I just had to find somewhere where Lizzie would feel comfortable. After making a few phone calls, I found an absolute beginner's class at a primary school only a bus ride away. Luckily I knew the teacher, Linda, so I was able to explain about Lizzie. She was very sympathetic, and I knew that the class would be perfect for Lizzie if she would go.

I decided to visit Lizzie at home instead of trying to see her in the school environment, even though a few curtains twitched when I arrived. Lizzie invited me into the neat and nicely decorated lounge where she still lived with her mum, who was drinking tea in the kitchen. I explained what I had arranged and held my breath.

"What do you think?" I enquired.

"It sounds good, but I'm really nervous about going," she replied, trembling.

"I'll go with you the first time if you want me to," I offered.

Lizzie considered this for a minute.

"No, I have to do this by myself. I have to find the courage," she whispered, "but thank you."

"Well done," I smiled at her, "come and tell me how you get on won't you?"

"Yes, sure I will," she answered.

The first class was in a couple of day's time so she didn't have long to worry about it.

"Don't know why you are bothering about this," came a voice from the lounge doorway. "It never did me any harm."

"Mum, I have tried to explain why to you, several times. It makes me unhappy that I can't join in things, and that I have to cover up the fact that I can't read or write, so please, let's not fall out about it again," said Lizzie, exasperatedly, trying to keep calm.

"You should be very proud of her, and give her all your support you know. She is being very brave," I exclaimed to the lady in the doorway, who just turned away and ignored me.

"Sorry about her," said Lizzie, embarrassed.

"No worries, I'd better be on my way, good luck," I replied. "See you."

"Cheers Sal," answered Lizzie, closing the door with a sad smile.

The days that followed were busy and full of surprises. Casey continued with her visits to Alcoholics Anonymous, and progressed well. She was thrilled when Ian decided to join her. She still enjoyed her English classes where she came up with something rather special. Her girls, Eva and Sophie, had got up early one morning and decided to do some baking on their own. They made an awful mess in the kitchen and Casey had decided to write about it. The English teacher was thrilled about what Casey had written.

Recipe for Disaster

Ingredients

Take two children preferably one called Sophie, the other called Eva.

Other essentials

A kitchen and a cupboard full of food.
To make the disaster happen take a lie-in on Sunday morning.
The children are mixed together with one loaf of bread, and a lump of butter spread on their heads.

A bag of sugar spread all over the floor.
A jar of jam thrown over the door.
A pack of eggs all trodden into the mat.
A jug of orange poured over the cat.
A pack of biscuits crushed into bits.
Treacle syrup smeared over their lips.
Give a good stir and sprinkle with flour.

Then leave to settle for at least an hour.
Takes two to three hours to clean!!!
"Casey, that's brilliant," I exclaimed.

"I was so mad when I found them, but then we saw the funny side to it all," she chuckled, "we did get them to help clean it up, but the mess got worse."

Mrs Harper appeared through the door-way. She often came across to see what was happening in the Room which always pleased them immensely.

"Mrs Harper, would you like to read my poem?" spluttered Casey, hardly able to contain herself.

"I should love to, thank you," answered Mrs Harper, taking hold of the printed page.

As she read it, a delightful smile flickered across her face.

"Casey, that is great, it ought to be published," she enthused, "thank you for sharing it with me."

An idea popped into my head as Casey stood there beaming with pride, and growing in stature by the minute. Mrs Harper had the knack of making everyone feel valued.

"Could I have a copy please?" I asked, "to show to my friends."

No sooner had I asked, there was a copy in my hand.

CHAPTER 12

Realisation

Jill Sykes and Janine were attending their Child Development course every Friday morning, and always came stomping back at lunchtime, muttering how hard it was, and why had I persuaded them to start it? Did I? I couldn't remember that - I soon learned to make myself scarce at Friday lunchtimes.

After a little thought I decided to put my idea with Casey's poem in action. I sent the poem with a covering letter to the Gazette, in the hope that they would be interested as they had already done an article on the Parents' Room. Whether it was right or not, I decided not to tell Casey or anybody about what I had done. If nothing came of it then no harm had been done, and nobody would be any the wiser.

Lizzie came to find me after her first reading and writing lesson at the primary school. I was in a side room off the corridor.

"I was so scared walking into a strange school," she said. "I felt as if everyone was staring at me, and it took me a while to ask the receptionist where the classroom was in case she thought I was stupid. I waited until there was nobody else around, but I needn't have worried because she was very nice and took me to the classroom. My heart was beating so loudly, I thought she would hear it. When we got to the classroom door I wanted the ground to swallow me up, as I was so nervous, and I knew my face was red and my mouth was so dry."

She stopped, Lizzie was talking as if she was re-living every nerve wracking second.

"And?" I enquired, gently.

"Sorry, yes, I walked into the classroom and saw six other faces looking just as nervous and strained as I was feeling. Anyway, Mrs Tilson our teacher, was brilliant and she introduced me to everyone. Then we sat and chatted for a few minutes about how we all felt – and they all felt like me!

It made me realise that I wasn't the only one in the whole wide world who couldn't read or write. Suddenly, I felt a weight lifting from me - I was able to share my feelings with like-minded people - a relief after hiding and bottling it up for so many years."

That was quite a speech from Lizzie and I could see a tear in her eyes.

"Lizzie, I am so proud of you," I exclaimed. "Well done!"

"I'm proud of myself," she replied, "and that feels good. I am going to do this, you know."

"Of course you will, and you will make new friends," I answered happily.

"Just got to convince Mum now," she commented.

"Try to understand your mum was brought up like that and doesn't know any difference. She may change her mind, just don't be hurt by any of her comments," I tried to explain.

"Yes, I know. Right, I must go, I've got some homework to do," she laughed, "ready for my next class."

With that she skipped off down the corridor.

The Room was busy and the English class was in full swing when the phone went, making everyone jump.

"Phone Sal," shouted Carol.

"I think she can hear it," Greta commented.

It was the Gazette ringing to say that they were interested in publishing Casey's poem, and could they come and take some photos of her and the girls. I was so thrilled for her, and then I remembered that I had not told her I had sent off the poem. Quietly I explained that, and asked if they would speak to Casey herself, which they said they would.

"Casey, it's for you," I called.

"Me? Who's ringing me?" she questioned.

"Come and see," I replied, smiling.

"What have you been up to?" she demanded.

"Just answer the phone, they won't wait forever," I said pushing the phone in her direction.

"Hello," said Casey. The room fell silent – even Carol.

"You are joking, really?" she exclaimed after a few seconds. "Yes, yes, that's fantastic, thank you. You had better arrange a time with Sally. Yes, see you soon, and thanks again."

She handed me the phone, grinning from ear to ear and clenching her fists together with delight. I arranged for the reporter to come the next day amid the din of excitement around me.

"My poem, my poem, I'm going to be published," said Casey, dancing with joy around the room. "It was the Gazette – when are they coming Sal?"

"Tomorrow morning at 10.30," I replied.

"Have we got to get dressed up?" asked Carol.

"No Dumbo, they are not coming to take pictures of you, it's Casey and her girls," retorted Greta.

"Oh well, it's *only* the local paper isn't it?" snapped back Carol, scowling.

"That's not a very nice thing to say, Carol," said Abbey. "We should be pleased for Casey. When have you been in the paper for something you have done?"

"I haven't, but I might be one day," sniffed Carol, sulkily. "I'm not good at anything."

"You have been in the paper, you know," commented Emma.

"When, I can't remember?" replied Carol.

"We all got dressed up and went collecting for Children in Need in town. You were dressed as Humpty Dumpy and had too much to drink, and you fell in the river and had to be rescued, if you remember," chuckled Emma.

"Oh yes," cackled Carol. "I knew I was good at something - collecting for charity."

Everyone had a giggle at the memory, and harmony was restored once more.

Even I had forgotten about that, I don't know how because I was there too!

CHAPTER 13

A Little Dusty

The next morning came all too quickly. Casey arrived early, with Eva and Sophie clutching a sheet and bag of flour.

"What on earth is that for?" asked Greta, handing out the coffee and sending ciggie ash everywhere.

"I thought if we could stand the girls on the sheet, and put flour in their hair, it would be fun for the photo. I've even brought some jam to dab on their noses," explained Casey.

"Blimey, the cleaners are going to love that," replied Greta, gruffly. "Oh God, look at me, I've still got my slippers on."

"We'll just have to be careful, but I'll clean it up if needs be," chattered Casey cheerfully. "What do you think, Sal?"

"I think it's a good idea, so long as we don't leave a mess," I answered.

"Don't let Carol near that bag of flour whatever you do," chortled Greta.

"Don't let me near what?" asked a gravelly voice coming into the room. "Flour and jam? Are we baking?"

"No we're not. We're, oh you explain Casey, time I went for the bingo prizes," chuntered Greta, "I won't be long, I want to see the pictures being taken," and with that Greta departed for Shabby Syd's.

"She's got her slippers on," chortled Carol, gleefully, "I'd better tell her."

Before anyone could tell Carol that Greta knew about the slippers, she opened the window and bawled at the top of her voice.

"You've got your slippers on Greta,"

With a two fingered wave, Greta acknowledged that she knew.

I had a couple of home visits to do, so I set off straight away so that I could be back before the people from the Gazette arrived.

There was some concern about Cassie's son, Dominic who was six years old. He had become withdrawn at times, but quick tempered with the other children and beginning to lash out at them. Cassie hadn't been into the Room for a few days which was unusual. She often sported a bruise on her face, but was always very reluctant to talk about it and just laughed it off.

I pulled up outside the end terraced house and noticed that the lounge curtains were drawn to, even though it was half past nine in the morning. Picking my way through the litter blowing on the drive, and the neglected front garden, I began to feel a little uneasy.

This was just not like Cassie at all. She always kept things clean and tidy. I knocked on the door and waited, but no-one answered. Instinctively I knew someone was inside. Knocking again, I shouted through the letter box,

"Cassie, it's me, Sally from school. Are you okay?"

"I'm fine thanks," came the reply.

Not convinced, I tried again.

"Just open the door so that I can see you are okay. This isn't like you Cassie. I'm worried about you," I called.

"No, go away Sally, please," came a tearful answer, "just leave me alone."

"Alright, but you're obviously not okay, and whatever it is, it's affecting Dominic and making him miserable and badly behaved. I've got to go now, but I shall come back tomorrow unless you come to see me," I shouted through the letter box.

As I turned to go, I heard the key click in the lock and the door opened ajar. Cautiously, I stepped inside the dimly lit hallway.

"Where are you Cassie," I asked.

"In here," came a sad voice from the lounge. "Be careful when you come in."

I pushed the door open and gasped at the sight before my eyes. The room was a total mess, the mirror was smashed, the TV was off its plinth, there were fist holes in the door and photographs were strewn all over the floor in their cracked frames. Cassie was sitting huddled on the settee in her dressing gown.

She began to cry, and her shoulders began to shake with emotion, as sobs racked through her small frame. I sat down next to her and put my arm round her shoulders.

"Sshh now, calm down and try and tell me what it is," I encouraged her.

"It's my own fault," she sobbed, wiping her nose and eyes on her dressing gown sleeve.

"How on earth is this mess your fault, did you do it?" I enquired.

"No I didn't," Cassie choked, "but I caused it."

"Cassie look at me and tell me exactly what this is about. This isn't like you, even the garden is a mess," I questioned.

Turning to look at me, I could see a nasty black eye and several fainter bruises on her face. Trying not to look horrified, I asked again what had happened.

"Well, I think you have guessed that I have been seeing someone else while Trev was away in the army," she admitted sniffing.

"I had thought something was going on, and I have seen bruises before, but you always laughed them off so I didn't pry," I answered.

"I know it's wrong," she continued, "but Trev has always been controlling in a way, and never hit me too hard, but he has worn me down over the years and I can't love him anymore. Then I met Barney in the Robin Hood when I was out with Carol and Janine one night. We got on so well, swapped phone numbers and it went on from there."

"How long has it been going on?" I asked.

"About eighteen months, and I know I shouldn't, but Barney is so kind and caring, and makes me feel wanted and valued. Please don't think badly of me Sal," she implored.

"No, I'm not here to judge you, I'm going to try and help," I replied.

"Three weeks ago I decided to tell Trev how I felt and come clean about Barney.

As I suspected, he knew deep down things weren't right, and he wasn't happy either," she explained. "He slapped me across my face and stormed out, and didn't come back for three days. The thing is Dominic saw it all and was so frightened poor kid. It was the first time he had hit me in front of him. So you see, it's all my fault."

"No man has any right to hit a woman, especially in front of a child," I retorted, feeling a sense of anger bubbling up.

"But I've provoked him Sal," she persisted.

"You may have done wrong, but that doesn't give him any excuse to hurt you, Cassie," I said firmly. "How did the rest of the damage happen, and that black eye looks new?"

"He left me alone until two days ago when he came back from the pub blind drunk in the afternoon. That's when he wrecked the place and he hit me again. He told me to be gone when he next came back on leave. He left yesterday and didn't even say goodbye to Dominic, which upset him, even though he was wary of him much of the time, he was his dad. So here I am, left in this mess and nowhere to go, but I am going somewhere," she declared with a growing determination.

"Does Dominic know about Barney?" I asked curiously.

"Yes, rightly or wrongly he does. He used to come to the house, but we were very discreet. Dom likes him very much," she smiled, "he makes us laugh."

"Does Barney know what's happened?" I asked.

"Yes, I spoke to him last night. He'll be coming into dock tonight – he's on the trawlers and lives in Devon," Cassie explained. "He's coming to see me this evening."

"Well, you had better get tidied up and get yourself sorted out then." I smiled, "and be gentle with Dominic. Now we know what's wrong I'll tell them at school, but don't worry, I won't go into detail."

"Okay, thanks Sal, better pull myself together," she grinned through red rimmed panda eyes, where her black mascara had run.

I glanced at my watch.

"Oh gosh, is that the time? I'd better fly, the photographers are coming to school, and I want to be there. Cheerio, come and let me know what's happening. Take care."

"I shall," Cassie called out as I headed for the door, picking my way through the glass on the carpet.

Walking through the Parents' Room door a sight hit my eyes. Standing on the sheet were Eva and Sophie, with flour all dusted in their hair, and jam smeared on their cheeks and noses.

The reporter and photographer were already there and were making clicking noises of approval.

"This is super, what a good idea to go with the poem," the young male photographer gushed, chuckling.

"Err, could we perhaps get the girls to throw flour up into the air?" the hippy looking female reporter asked tentatively.

Mrs Harper came into the room at this point to see what was going on.

"The young lady has asked if the girls could throw flour up in the air." I said to Mrs Harper, not knowing what she would think.

"What a wonderful idea," she cried.

"Who's going to sweep up the mess?" bemoaned Carol.

"You know where the brushes and vacuum are kept," replied Mrs Harper, smiling at Carol. "Right come on girls, dip your hands into the flour bag, and throw it above your heads."

The two young girls dipped their hands into the bag in front of them.

"One, two, three throw," shouted our fun loving Head Teacher, enjoying every minute. Eva and Sophie threw the flour and the photographer clicked rapidly as clouds of flour went everywhere.

"It's different to ciggie smoke, makes a change," chortled Greta, coughing and wafting the dust with her hands, scattering ciggie ash everywhere.

"That was fun," cried Casey, "now we had better clean up. Get the vacuum Carol please,"

"I didn't make the mess," grumbled Carol, "but it's been fun so I suppose I could help."

"Do you think it might be a good idea to take the girls home and get them cleaned up, it is almost lunchtime," suggested Mrs Harper to Casey.

"Oh can I, thanks? No, I think I'll clear up here first." smiled Casey.

"No, you get off, I'll clear up here," exclaimed Carol, grinning that toothy grin.

"Carol you are a funny old thing," said Casey, "thanks."

"But you love me, don't you?" chortled Carol.

Casey took the girls home, the reporter and photographer left, still laughing, and in no time at all the room was clean – we thought.

Mrs Harper helped and then stopped to have a coffee with everyone which they loved.

Bingo went well in the afternoon, except the prizes were coated in flour dust, much to Greta's amusement.

CHAPTER 14
Happy Ever After

The first person through the door next morning was Cassie! She still looked tired and drawn and had plenty of make-up on to disguise her bruises, but they were still in evidence.

"How are you?" I asked quietly.

"Much better thanks," she replied smiling. "I'll tell you all about it later, other people are arriving now, and they don't want to hear about my problems."

"You'd be surprised, problem shared and all that," I answered.

Greta arrived, grabbed a coffee and sat down in an easy chair with gusto, and sent a cloud of flour dust into the air.

"Did you fart when you sat down Greta?" cackled Carol, "you made a right puff of flour."

"No I bloody didn't," chuntered Greta, "if you had cleaned up properly yesterday, that wouldn't have happened. I had it all in my bingo prizes."

"Sorry, that's all my fault," exclaimed Casey. "I'll go round and dust everything when it's quieter."

"Hiya Cassie, we've not seen you for a while. What door have you walked into this time?" observed Carol in her most tactful way.

"Carol, don't be so nosey," Emma said, "maybe Cassie doesn't want to talk about it."

Unabashed, Carol sat down next to Cassie to scrutinise her face more closely.

Cassie looked uncomfortable, and looked to me for support.

"Carol, Cassie doesn't want you in her face, please," I requested.

"I was only trying to be friendly," retorted Carol, backing off.

"Nosey more like it," muttered Greta under her breath.

"No, it's okay. I didn't walk into a door. Trev did it and he smashed up the house as well. He and I are finished, I can't take any more of his bullying," gabbled Cassie, taking a gulp of breath.

She didn't offer any more information, and the rest of the room made their sympathetic noises of support and understanding.

One of the Nursery staff was off for the afternoon and I was requested to cover for her, and I hadn't had time to talk to Cassie and find out her news. I was in the wet area with the water tray, sand and painting easels for the afternoon – the perfect combination for making a mess.

Cassie wandered into the Nursery about two o'clock.

"I need to talk to you," she whispered, "now."

"I can't now Cassie, I'm sorry. Will it wait until home time?" I asked.

"No, I can't wait," she implored. "Barney wants me to go back with him to Devon and live there. I don't know what to do. Please help me."

A jet of water shot over my head and landed on the floor.

"Ben, don't do that, stop blowing the pipe so hard," I said. "Why is it so urgent that it can't wait?"

"Because I've got to go tonight if I'm going," Cassie replied, as yet another jet of water shot across the wet area and splattered onto Helen's painting.

"Ben! Stop it! Helen, stop that noise, I'll give you some new paper," I croaked.

"Trev is threatening to come home tomorrow and says woe-betide me if I'm still in the house," Cassie continued, following me to the painting easel while I changed Helen's paper. "Pleeseee tell me what to do."

"I can't, you have to make the decision yourself," I whispered frantically.

"David, why have you thrown the sand in the water tray?" I demanded of the four year old boy. "Oh I see, because Ben tipped a bucket of water into the sand tray. Ben get out of the water tray, now!"

Cassie looked at me with imploring eyes, and I knew I had to say something before the wet area deteriorated into complete chaos!!

"Do you love him?" I asked.

"Yes I do," answered Cassie, without hesitation,

"And Dominic likes him?"

"Yes."

"Well, there's your answer – go, and be happy ever after." I smiled at this lost little soul, who I knew would be okay.

A smile lit up her face.

"Thanks Sal," she said softly, "take care," and with a warm hug, she was gone.

As another jet of water shot over the wet area, a warm feeling came over me.

"Good luck Cassie," I whispered.

"Ben, what did I say to you? Oh never mind, you can stay in the water."

The young boy shot me a muddled look as if to say "It's about time she made her mind up."

When I went back to the Room after school had ended, Casey was still polishing and hoovering. She took the cushions outside to bang all the flour dust out of them.

"Did Cassie find you?" she asked. "She seemed quite agitated."

"Yes," I replied with a smile.

"What's making you smile like that?" she asked.

"I can't tell you at the moment, but you will find out eventually," I answered.

"Ohh secrets," chuckled Casey. "By the way, I am thinking about becoming a counsellor."

"Wow Casey, that's great," I exclaimed, "when do you start?"

"Next week if I go for it," she said, "and I think I shall."

As Casey left and made her way home, I sat quietly on my own. The Room could feel incredibly calm when it was empty, which wasn't very often. Altogether it had been a really rewarding day, if somewhat chaotic at times.

A week later, Casey charged into the Room waving a copy of the Gazette.

"It's in! My poem and the girls," she cried. "I've got you a copy Sal."

"Thanks, that's great, I'll treasure it," I answered, and I did.

CHAPTER 15

Christmas is Coming

Christmas was fast approaching and there was the usual, frantic decoration making, and chocolate logs occupied every child proof space available, ready to be taken home and frozen. Jill and Janine were still finding their Child Development course tough going, but they were determined to stick at it. Ian and Casey still attended the Alcoholic Anonymous meetings and were doing well. They had their lapses, but were drinking far less than they had done before. Casey had started her training course to become a counsellor and was really enjoying the challenge. I received a postcard from Cassie in Devon. On it were two words - 'thank you'. That was all I needed to know that she was fine, because I had worried about her. Lizzie was progressing well with her English lessons, but it was still a secret.

The best news of all was that Pete's wife Chris had been given the all clear from breast cancer. Emma baked a cake, and with permission we had a bottle of bubbly to celebrate.

Then I heard the dreaded words – what panto are we doing this year? I thought they may give it a miss this year, but no chance. They loved the opportunity to create their own costumes and get dressed up, and best of all they enjoyed entertaining the children.

After much discussion, they decided to perform Cinderella. Greta quickly cast herself as the Fairy Godmother, and Carol took great offence when someone suggested she played one of the ugly sisters. It was decided that Casey should be Cinderella, and Andy should be Prince Charming.

"And we are not having flipping Lycra gold tights this year," chortled Greta, "and no swearing our Carol."

"You swore too," chuckled Carol.

"Only because you did," sniggered Greta, "can you remember the expression on that po-faced teacher?"

Everyone laughed at the memories of last year's panto. I tried to look as if I wasn't listening about po-faced teachers – they were quite right though, it was so funny.

Pete was going to be Buttons, and Emma and Chris were going to play the Ugly Sisters, with Carol being the wicked Step-mother. Abbey, Janine and Sara offered to sort the scenery out and to be extras in the panto.

As the list went up for people to sign up for Christmas Dinner, Reverend Metcalf came to visit. She was a jolly person and they all enjoyed her company.

"I know you are busy, but I have a favour to ask. If it is going to be too much you must say," she said.

"Go on, what is it?" I replied, rather intrigued.

"Well you know I take the services at Brownhill village church," she continued, "The parishioners are mainly elderly and were saying that they miss the children from the village now that most of them had grown up and moved away. The village children used to put on the Nativity play in the church at Christmas, but of course that has not happened for years, and I was wondering...."

"If we could do a Nativity play," I finished her sentence.

"Yes, that's about it," she smiled, "in a nutshell."

"Oh gosh, I don't really know if we can," I replied lamely, thoughts whirling round my head.

Reverend Metcalf had been so good to us conducting the baptism in school.

"Well, what does everyone else think?" I commented, as I realised that they had all heard the request.

"I think it's a great idea," responded Sara, "I'll help."

"We have got enough children between us, and other parents will join in if we need any extras," commented Abbey.

"Come on Sal, say we'll do it. It will be fun and the kids will love it," added Janine.

How far these individuals had come was amazing. Their self-confidence had grown so much, and they all believed in themselves, so who was I to say no.

"Okay, as long as you all pull together and help. It's going to be a lot of hard work," I replied tentatively.

"Oh wonderful, thank you so much. The villagers will be so pleased," enthused Reverend Metcalf. "Thanks for the coffee. I'll wait to hear from you to finalise details. Bye for now."

"Bye" came the chorus from around the room as she departed.

"Don't look so worried Sal," said Casey. "How about we sort out which child is going to do what in the Nativity between ourselves, and then we run it past you?"

"Alright, but please no arguing," I answered smiling. "You will have to get a move on, there's not much time and there's the costumes to sort out."

"We can quickly run up some costumes in the sewing class if we need to," commented Lizzie, who had just come in and joined in the conversation.

"Oh dear, what have we taken on?" I thought to myself as they began to throw their ideas about. I went home that night with my head full of panto characters, Nativity ideas and Christmas dinner fare.

CHAPTER 16

The Nativity

It was decided that the Nativity would be performed on the Sunday evening before Christmas, when school would have broken up, and both panto and Christmas dinner would be out of the way. Despite my misgivings, events seemed to be quite organised!

As usual, there was very little rehearsing for the panto, but the show went very well, and everyone had a great afternoon's entertainment. Even the po-faced teacher looked as if she had half enjoyed herself.

Christmas dinner went as smoothly as possible – it never failed to amaze me how they managed to produce such a feast for so many people on just a Baby Belling cooker and microwave oven.

The term ended and I breathed a sigh of relief – just the Nativity to go now. True to their word, they had pretty much organised the play themselves, the sewing machines had gone into overdrive making costumes for the Shepherds, Wise Men and Angels. They were taken home to be pressed and final touches added.

There had been one rehearsal at church which I couldn't go to, but Reverend Metcalf reported that it had gone well.

Sunday evening came and I must admit that I was feeling rather nervous – should I have had more input and given them more guidance? I was meeting them at the church just after five for the service to start at six. As I pulled up at the church, I could see some of them arriving in their cars, and others coming on foot, clutching their costumes against the breeze. There was a short cut to the church across the playing fields, so the village was not too far from the estate.

"Hi Sal," chirped a gravelly voice through the darkness.

"Hi Carol, are you okay?" I replied.

"Yes, great, I am looking forward to this," she called.

I opened the heavy wooden door and entered the small church, and a wonderful scene met my eyes. In one corner, stood a beautiful Christmas tree, sparkling with gold and silver decorations, and white lights twinkling from top to bottom.

Candles lit the church with a soft warm glow, gently illuminating the lovely stained glass windows. Looking towards the altar I gaped in amazement – someone had built a stable, complete with straw bales.

"Do you like it?" asked a voice nearby.

Turning to look I saw Pete standing there, grinning.

"You've done that?" I asked, admiringly.

"Yes with a few mates helping me," replied Pete proudly. "Abbey painted the background animals."

"Pete, it's lovely, well done," I exclaimed. "I just never expected this."

"Well, you know what you always say- if a job is worth doing, do it well," he chuckled.

"And my, you have done it well," I replied.

There was a lot of giggling going on behind the red velvet curtains at the back of the church. I peeped through the curtains and saw a hive of activity. There were angel wings flapping and tinsel head dresses wobbling.

"Anyone need a hand?" I asked, feeling redundant.

"Please," said Casey, "I can't get Sophie's cloak to stay on."

Sophie was playing Mary and looked a picture in her blue dress. I managed to secure her cloak with some strategically placed hair grips. The shepherds had their tea towels fastened on their heads with cloth bands, and the Wise Men looked resplendent in their shiny robes and bejewelled crowns. It's amazing what you can do with Quality Street wrappers! I was so proud of them, they had all made such an effort with the costumes. Why did I worry?

The small church was beginning to fill up with eager parishioners, and there was a buzz all round.

"Do you want me to help during the performance?" I enquired.

"No, we want you to sit and enjoy it," said Greta, appearing from somewhere.

"Okay, if you are sure," I replied.

"Yes we are. Now buzz off and make yourself useful talking to the congregation," said Greta.

"Yes Ma'am," I chuckled, "right away."

I mingled with the parishioners who were obviously looking forward to the production.

"This is exciting," said Reverend Metcalf, breezing up. "Come on, there's a seat for you on the front row."

"Oh, I can't sit on the front row," I exclaimed.

"Yes you can, then the children will be able to see someone they know," replied Reverend Metcalf busily, ushering me to the front of the church.

On the dot of six, she stood up and addressed the congregation. There was the sound of sshh from behind the curtains, which made me smile.

"Welcome everybody, and a special welcome to those from the Meadows Infant and Nursery School."

"That's us," chirped a young voice "Sshh", there were some chuckles from the parishioners.

"As I was saying," the minister continued, "the children from the school are going to perform the Nativity play for us tonight."

Reverend Metcalf took her seat next to me and silence descended over the church. The strains of Little Donkey filled the church as Mary and Joseph made their way slowly down the aisle. Someone was making very authentic clip clops, I suppose with coconut halves.

As they reached the stable, Joseph pretended to knock on the door – there was knock, knock, knock, knock from behind the curtains. The Innkeeper emerged from behind the stable with his lantern swinging erratically from side to side.

"Is there any room at your inn?" asked Joseph. "Mary is about to have a baby."

"We have no room at the inn, but you can use the stable if you don't mind the animals," the Innkeeper said, pointing to the stable.

Mary and Joseph made their way without mishap onto the straw bales and sat on the small wooden stools.

"Thank you Innkeeper," said Joseph. "Try to get some sleep Mary."

Mary scrunched up her face, and closed her eyes tightly. I turned to look as the angels made their way down the aisle. They looked a picture as the candles flickered gently and reflected against their gold wings and sparkling halos.

They began to sing Twinkle Twinkle Little Star as they approached the stable. The last angel, Gabriel, who had a silver halo, was clutching a 'baby' in her arms. They carefully made their way and stood on the bench behind Mary and Joseph. Angel Gabriel shook Mary on the shoulder and shouted, "Wake up," which made us all jump and smile at the same time.

"I am the Angel Gabriel, and you have a new baby," she bellowed, "here he is and he is called Jesus."

Gabriel plonked the baby on Mary's knee and turned and beamed at everybody, before making her way to join the other angels on the bench. We had another chorus of Twinkle Twinkle from the angels as they held their hands together as if they were saying their prayers. Mary cradled baby Jesus in her arms and looked towards me and took a deep breath. I didn't know what was coming next, but I smiled and nodded encouragingly.

Mary (Sophie) began to sing Away in a Manger all by herself. Her voice wavered slightly, but then her young sweet voice filled the little church. Tears threatened to fill my eyes, and I could see people dabbing theirs. She gave a huge sigh of relief and sagged on her stool as she finished the verse. Everyone then joined in to sing the final verses.

Mary placed the baby in the wooden crib in front of her.

"Look, look, we have visitors coming to see us. It's the shepherds," bawled Gabriel, waking us all up and pointing down the aisle.

Trundling down the aisle came four shepherds with one carrying a lamb. As they walked along, there was a loud BAA BAA which sounded more like a strangled cat. I suspected it was Carol. The shepherds laid the lamb near the crib and sat down in front of Mary and Joseph.

"Oh God, look MORE visitors," shouted Gabriel, putting in more vocal effort than ever. "It's the WISE MEN!"

There were smiles in the congregation.

The Wise Men walked slowly and sedately down the aisle, clutching their precious gifts for Baby Jesus.

"I bring you gold," said the first Wise Man.

"I bring you frankincense," said the second.

"I bring you myrrh," said the third.

When they had all put their gifts down, they bowed and knelt down opposite the shepherds. Then, with the aid of a recording, the children sang "Twas on a starry night, when the world was bright," which tells the story of the birth of Jesus in a carol.

It was my favourite carol and I was struggling to keep my emotions under control. Music has always had that effect on me, and still does to this day.

As the carol ended Sara came to the front of the church. I could not believe my eyes – Sara!! She faced the congregation, smiled and confidently said, "That is the end of our Nativity play. We all hope that you have enjoyed watching it, as much as we have enjoyed performing it for you. Thank you."

Reverend Metcalf stood up and led the very warm and enthusiastic applause.

I thought my heart would burst with pride, as all the parents came from behind the curtains to applaud their children.

"Thank you, thank you so much for that wonderful performance," cried Reverend Metcalf happily. "We shall look forward to the next one with joy."

I then realised that we had set a precedent!

The children, parents and congregation all mingled together, laughing and talking, which was nice to see. There was mulled wine, sausage rolls and mince pies for the grown-ups, and lemonade and fairy cakes for the children.

"I could get used to this mulled wine – never had it before," commented Carol, grinning happily.

"Steady on Carol, don't overdo it," I replied.

"No, I won't, did you like my lamb imitation?" asked Carol.

"Yes, I thought it was you," I said wryly, "it was very unusual."

"The lamb had a sore throat," cackled Carol.

I spotted Sara sitting on the bench in the stable and decided to join her.

"Well, who would have thought it? Just look how far you have come. You were so brave, speaking in front of everyone. I am so proud of you," I told her.

"Do you know Sal, I was shaking like a leaf, but I was determined to do it, and I am proud of myself," she replied, smiling.

"So you should be," I said, putting my arm round her giving her a hug.

It was so rewarding seeing individuals believe and value themselves – it made it all so worthwhile.

After wishing everyone 'Happy Christmas', I departed. I wondered as I drove home what the next term would bring. In this job you just didn't know what was round the next corner.

The Christmas holiday began with a frenzied shopping spree for presents, followed by yards of wrapping paper and sellotape being administered.

As usual, I was icing the family Christmas cake at the last minute, before our traditional family get together on Christmas Day. There was usually a fair sized gathering, all enjoying the fun of beetle drive in the evening. Boxing Day brought the local derby football match, usually freezing cold. Inevitably, at these local games, the hooligan element from both teams thought it was fun to cause chaos. They just chased each other first one way, and then the other – I suppose it was their way of keeping warm. The match was usually an anti-climax, with the usual barracking and complaining about the match officials. One of the funniest comments I heard, aimed at the official after one particularly bad display was, "Referee, you are an oxygen thief, a complete oxygen thief."

I often encountered parents from school, usually dads, who always looked surprised to see me at the matches.

CHAPTER 17

Two Daft Prats

The first day of the spring term dawned. As usual, Greta was there before I arrived and always had a mug of tea waiting for me. I had great affection for Greta – we had struck up a friendship and an understanding from the first day we had met.

"Hi Greta, good Christmas?" I asked.

"Not bad thanks. I went to Andy's for Christmas dinner with everyone else. There were twenty three adults and God knows how many children," replied Greta gruffly.

"Goodness me, that's a house full," I exclaimed.

"It was but we all mucked in. It was chaos but good fun," she said, smiling at the memory. "I was pleased to get home in the evening though."

"I bet you were," I chuckled. "Any nice presents?"

"Oh God, that was a laugh I got six pairs of slippers," she chortled, "and they were all different. Still, I do get through lots of them. I ended up in town wearing them the other day. I realised that when I was on the bus!"

"Oh Greta, what are you like?" I smiled as the others started to arrive, chatting excitedly and swapping Christmas stories.

When the initial buzz had settled down, we discussed what different talks etc. they would like - English, Maths and sewing were ongoing.

"How about a keep fit and relaxation classes again?" suggested Lizzie, doing her stretching exercises.

Quite a few of the others nodded their heads in approval.

"Count me out on that one," said Greta, "it takes me all my time to get my draws on in the morning."

"What do you fancy then Greta?" asked Casey laughing.

"Bet you there's a lot she fancies, but she's not going to tell us," chipped in Carol, grinning her toothy grin.

"You cheeky bugger," retorted Greta, smiling. "How about a talk from the Citizens' Advice Bureau?"

Everyone agreed that would be interesting, plus some craft classes for making things for the Spring or Easter Fair at school.

"I think that's enough to be going on with," I suggested.

We already had quite a busy timetable, and groups still attended the senior school for netball and swimming, and we must not forget the bingo!

The phone shrilled in the Room, making us all jump. It was the secretary.

"Can you come along to Mrs Harper's office please?"

"Okay, I'll be there in a minute," I replied.

"Are you going on a home visit?" asked Carol.

"No, I'm not, and anyway it's none of your business what I'm doing, Miss Nosey," I said, pretending to be annoyed, which didn't work as Carol just cackled with laughter.

I made my way around the edge of the hall, trying to avoid soft bouncy balls and bean bags flying through the air during a Nursery PE lesson.

I tapped on Mrs Harper's door and went into her office.

Doreen was sitting there in the comfy chair, resplendent in a pink and white polka dot headscarf, with the usual sponge rollers protruding from the front.

"Hi Doreen, how are you?" I enquired, "not seen you for a while"

"Not good," she spluttered, "Our Lisa's kids have been flaying up and tetting into trouble, and it's tetting me down - she is popeless."

Doreen clutched her head with a hand in a dramatic fashion and fanned her face with the other hand, her speech impediment surfacing

"I'm going to paint in a minute, I just know I am," she cried, flopping back into the chair.

"Can I get you a drink of water?" enquired Mrs Harper, smiling wryly at me.

"Yes flease," sniffed Doreen.

Mrs Harper produced a glass of water from the water machine.

"Now calm down, take a deep breath and tell us what the matter is," I said.

"Our Jane won't go to the beech with her mother, so I'm going to take her tomorrow, so I'm just letting you know." explained Doreen, slurping the water.

"But why are you taking her to the beach at this time, it will be very cold? Not the weather for making sand-castles," I asked, puzzled.

"No no, to the beech, the beech," Doreen said exasperatingly, spraying water everywhere, her rollers wobbling precariously. "It's to help her pork roperly."

"Oh, the speech therapist," I said, the penny dropping at last.

"That's what I said," Doreen said, peering over her glasses at us both as if we were daft. I daren't look at Mrs Harper.

"It's very good of you to take her, just tell her teacher what time you will be back, and she will get her mark for dinner," explained Mrs Harper to Doreen.

"I will, fank you, pest to be toing," announced Doreen, departing down the corridor.

"It's okay, you can laugh now," chortled Mrs Harper.

"Oh dear, poor Doreen. That daughter of hers leads her a merry dance, and the more she gets worked up, the worse her speech impediment gets," I laughed.

Sometimes you had to laugh in this job to keep sane. It wasn't being unkind, it was just called self-preservation!!

Wendy the secretary popped her head round the door and laughingly asked,

"What have you said to Doreen? She's gone down the corridor muttering about two daft prats"

CHAPTER 18

Records of Achievement

Life ticked along quite quietly for a while. It was nice to see so many parents helping in the classrooms, and the Nursery. They were not all from the Parents' Room – not everybody felt comfortable coming into the Room and that was fine. The helpers were mainly mums, and females from the community, but there were a couple of dads who came in to help which was great.

Mrs Harper asked me if I would visit a school across the bridge to check out a new idea called Records of Achievement that she had heard about. She suggested that I took a couple of parents with me to see what they thought. Casey and Lizzie were able to come with me, although Lizzie was rather apprehensive.

"What if I have to read something I can't understand?" she asked nervously.

"You'll be fine," I assured her, "you are doing great, aren't you, just stick with me."

"Yes, I'm really improving," she answered proudly.

"Well then, stop worrying," I smiled.

We arrived at Carr Hill primary school and were made very welcome by everybody, and ushered into the Nursery where the Records of Achievement were introduced.

We each sat with a group of children who showed us their Record of Achievement file. Each child had a clip file which was filled with photos, certificate, stickers and pieces of work which recorded the child's individual stage of development. For example: "I learned how to write my name today" or "I know my colours" and each piece was dated by the teacher. The files were left at school during the week, and then taken home on Friday for parents or carers to look at and add their own contributions. This was a complete partnership between home and the school for the child. It was obvious that the children loved their files as they took such enjoyment showing them to us, and then talking about their contents. There were mums helping who were equally thrilled with them. Looking through I noticed that most parents had added something to their child's file.

Thanking the Head Teacher, we took our leave and headed for home, full of enthusiasm.

"They are great," said Casey, "I should love one of those."

"Me too," added Lizzie, "and I could read most of it."

Lizzie went bright red when she realised what she had said in front of Casey.

"That's great," exclaimed Casey, "well done you!"

"Oh...did you know I can't read and write very well?" stammered Lizzie.

"Well, yes, I sort of guessed," admitted Casey. "You used to avoid reading anything or you listened carefully to what we were saying and picked things up."

"Do the others know?" enquired Lizzie, sounding worried.

"No, no-one has mentioned it, and I haven't said anything," replied Casey.

"Thank goodness for that," exclaimed Lizzie, "I get so embarrassed."

"It's nothing to be ashamed of you know," said Casey, sympathetically.

"Lizzie has been going to another school to learn how to read and write," I explained.

"That's really brave of you," observed Casey.

"The worst part was plucking up courage to tell someone, but I told Sal and she arranged everything for me. The only person who knew was my mum, and she thought it was a waste of time my learning. She can't read or write so she couldn't see why I wanted to," chattered Lizzie, suddenly opening up and sounding quite at ease telling Casey all about it.

They talked happily all the way back to school about all sorts of things, but especially the Record of Achievement files.

I reported back to Mrs Harper and Lizzie and Casey also gave their opinions.

"Well Sal, what do you think?" asked Mrs Harper, when we were on our own.

"I don't think we really have a choice. I think they will go down a storm," I replied.

"It's half-term in two weeks time. Shall we introduce them the first week after that?" suggested our leader. "We've got time to order files and stickers."

"Any ideas how we are going to do it?" I enquired.

"We can introduce the parents to it by having meetings every morning, class by class. You'll be able to manage that won't you?"

"Me? You want me to do it?" I exclaimed.

"Well, who else?" beamed Mrs Harper, patting me on the shoulder. "Right, I'll get the files and sticker packs ordered tomorrow."

Half-term went in a flash, and I returned to boxes full of files, stickers and plastic envelopes.

Each file had a pack of 'I can do' stickers and plastic envelopes, and it took all of the in-service day to assemble them ready for the forthcoming 'workshops' with the parents. The Nursery groups were attending first, and then the five classes in the school. The top class was not joining in because they only had a half-term to go before they left for the Junior School. It had been decided to charge fifty pence for each file.

I waited pensively in the spare classroom for the parents of the Red and Blue Nursery groups to join me, hoping that they would like the idea and take it on board. They arrived in dribs and drabs after dropping their children off at the Nursery. Some of them were chatting happily, but others were looking a little apprehensive, wondering what was coming.

To my delight, every parent turned up or sent someone to represent them if they couldn't make it. The idea was met with mainly enthusiasm, although a few looked a little doubtful. Everyone left clutching a file, looking at them with curiosity. Each meeting was the same and I could sense a growing buzz around the school.

On the Friday morning of the first week of meetings, I was walking down the corridor when I heard the sound of running feet. I turned to tell the culprit off for running, and was almost bowled over by one of the mums, who I vaguely recognised.

"Sorry, sorry," she gasped, "but I don't want to miss out."

"It's okay, miss out on what?" I questioned.

"The files, my meeting isn't until next week, but I want to leave my fifty pence deposit to make sure I get one," she spluttered. "Celia will never forgive me; she's going on about them all the time."

"Oh bless you," I smiled, "don't worry, there's a file for every child."

"Are you sure," she said. "Please take my fifty pence, just to set my mind at rest."

"Alright, if you insist," I laughed, taking the coin from a sweaty hand, "I'll make a note of it."

"Thank you so much," she replied. "See you next week." And off she went with a spring in her step.

If I ever had any doubts about the Records of Achievement being a success, they just disappeared down the corridor.

CHAPTER 19

Let's go on a Coach Trip

The spring term flew by, and before I knew it there were chocolate Easter eggs, made in the craft classes, adorning the shelves in the Parents' Room. Talks and classes had gone well, Jill and Janine were plodding on with their Child Development course, Lizzie was enjoying her English classes and growing in confidence, and Casey was doing well with her counselling course. Greta was busy organising her Easter coach trip to Scarborough and had nearly filled the usual three coaches.

"There's a couple of seats left on the third coach," Greta mentioned. "Do you fancy a trip to Scarborough?"

She looked at me, expectantly.

I realised how much she wanted me to go, and I hadn't been on a trip for a while.

"Okay, I'll see if my friend Judy wants to go," I replied, "I'll let you know tomorrow."

"Okay Sal, it would be nice if you could come with us," she said.

I rang Judy that night.

"How about coming to Scarborough on a coach trip, and meet all the people I tell you about in person?" I asked.

"That will be great, thanks. I shall really look forward to that," cried Judy.

She loved hearing about the people I worked with. I was always very discreet, and I knew that Judy would not repeat anything that she shouldn't.

Greta looked as pleased as punch when I told her we wanted to join them. The trip was on the first Sunday after the school had broken up. I picked Judy up and we drove to meet the coaches outside Shabby Syd's. I left my car in Emma's drive which was just round the corner.

Quite a crowd had gathered, and they were all chatting excitedly, waiting for the coaches to arrive. Much to my delight, Sarah and Abbey were going on the trip with their children for the first time. They had developed a very close friendship and supported each other all the time.

"Hi Sal," came a chorus of voices.

"Hi everybody, this is my friend Judy," I replied.

"Hi Judy," came a similar chorus, making Judy smile.

"Hello everyone, lovely to meet you. I've heard so much about you," called Judy.

"Well, who am I then?" cackled a voice nearby.

"Carol, don't be rude to Sal's friend," commented Emma.

"You're Carol and you've got a little girl called Chloe." replied Judy

Everyone laughed, and for once Carol looked slightly abashed and speechless.

"How did you remember she had a daughter called Chloe?" I whispered.

"I recognised her from your description," Judy replied, giggling.

The three coaches arrived, and Greta arrived with her family in tow and a list clutched in her hand.

"Right," she said, "coach one, first on Sal and Judy – front seat."

"I thought we were on coach three," I protested.

"No, coach one," she repeated, looking sternly at me.

"Best get on and do as we are told," I said to Judy, and clambered up the steps to sit in the allocated front seats. It took about fifteen minutes to load the coaches, and when everybody was on board, Greta climbed onto our coach and sat in the seat opposite Judy and me.

"Do you always tell them which coach they are on?" I asked Greta.

"Yes, I make sure that everyone gets on with the people on their coach. We don't want any trouble and get a bad reputation," she explained.

"Amazing," whispered Judy, "she must know all the families inside out."

"She's been running trips for years, so she does know what's she is doing." I replied, feeling very proud to know Greta, and realising how much people on the estate looked up to her and respected her.

"Right, let's roll," called Graham, our coach driver. "Are we ready darl?" he asked Greta.

"There's just Doreen and her friend to come, but they are very late," replied Greta, glancing at her watch with a very bright, pink strap. "I guess we had better set off, we can't wait all day. They are probably in the middle of a family bust-up knowing them."

"Here we go folks," cried Greta, clapping her hands and sending ciggie ash everywhere.

There was a collective cheer as Graham started the engine.

"Hang on Greta, Doreen has just come round the corner," called a voice from the back of the coach.

"Oh my God!" exclaimed Greta, rolling her eyes. "What the bloody hell are they doing on those things?"

I looked out of the coach window and struggled to suppress hysterical laughter.

Doreen and her friend Gladys were coming round the corner at full tilt on two disabled motorised scooters.

One was red and the other was blue. Doreen's two protruding hair rollers were bouncing up and down like a yo-yo, peeping out from under her bright, yellow chiffon scarf.

Gladys was sporting a large straw hat, which she had to keep holding on as she sped along, even though it was fastened by red ribbons under her chin. I glanced at Judy who was looking on in disbelief.

"Welcome to my world," I said to her, as we both started to laugh.

Judy and I had the same sense of humour, and didn't have to say anything to each other if an amusing situation arose – we just laughed.

As Doreen and Gladys drew alongside the coaches, Doreen managed to stop her scooter with a jerk. Her bag, which had been on the floor at her feet, flew off and its contents rolled under the coach. Gladys however didn't stop.

"Pop, pop you daft cow, put the skates on," we could hear Doreen shouting.

That did it for Judy, and she collapsed in her seat giggling helplessly. Gladys didn't stop, and continued for a few more yards before losing her hat and control of the scooter, and got wedged in a thick overgrown privet hedge. By now, everyone on the coach was having a good laugh at their expense.

"What the frigging hell are you doing?" bawled Greta, climbing down the coach steps.

"I'd better go and help." I said to Judy, who still didn't know where to put herself for laughing.

"Doreen, why are you on a scooter?" I enquired trying to keep a straight face. "Well, we heard that Scarborough is pull if pills, and fort we would be fetter on these," Doreen spluttered.

"Where have you got them from?" asked Greta, as Gladys arrived pushing her scooter, helped by some passers-bye who had pulled her out of the hedge. Her straw hat was perched at an angle on her head and her bright red lipstick was smeared over her chin and nose, giving her a clown like appearance.

"I told you we shouldn't have trusted those lads, Dor. The stupid brakes didn't work on mine," Gladys grumbled. "Some lads down the road said we could hire them for a tenner a day, and this dizzy dope fell for it."

"Don't you fall me a spizzy frope," shouted Doreen, crossly.

"Okay, calm down both of you," said Greta. "Are you both alright?"

"My papples are under the poach," muttered Doreen, sulkily.

"Never mind moaning about your apples. You are making us very late. You can buy some chips in Scarborough!" retorted Greta.

"What if she doesn't want any chips?" called a voice from an open coach window.

"If you don't shut up Carol, you'll be off the coach," said Greta, trying to keep calm in the face of adversity. "Right, on the coach, both of you."

"What about our pooters?" enquired Doreen.

That was the final straw.

"I'm not having those bloody dodgy scooters on my coach outing," shouted Greta, "If you two are coming, get on the coach NOW!"

"Alright, keep your pair on," muttered Doreen.

"Leave it Greta," I whispered, as I could see that Greta was going to fire back with both barrels. "Let's get off and have a lovely day."

"Yes, you're right. Whatever will your friend think of us all?" replied Greta.

"What Judy? She'll be loving every minute," I answered with a grin.

With peace restored, and Doreen and Gladys safely on board, the three coaches set off for Scarborough in convoy.

The journey there was pretty uneventful. There was the usual passing round of the name cards, with which half of the proceeds went to the winner, and the other half went to the driver's fish and chips for lunch. There was the occasional muttering from Doreen announcing that she was hungry and could just eat a papple.

We arrived at our destination at lunch time, and everyone went their separate ways with friends and family. The weather was lovely, so Judy and I went for a stroll down the beach, and then found a quiet pub for lunch.

It was good to spend time together. We had met years ago at my first teaching job, and Judy had returned to teaching after having a family, and we had been close friends ever since. She was a tremendous support when my first marriage broke up, and had helped and guided me through 'the dark days'. We finished our lunch and wandered round the seaside town, every now and then waving to people from our coaches. Carol emerged from a fortune teller's booth looking very pleased with herself for some reason that I'm sure we shall all hear about sooner or later.

"Hi Sal," called a voice.

It was Greta and some of her family, sitting at a table outside a café. They were all enjoying ice-creams in the warm sunshine, and a balmy breeze that was just beginning to blow. Judy and I went to join them.

"Guess what?" she said chuckling.

"Don't tell me you came in your slippers," I replied.

"Yes I did," she laughed gleefully, waving a foot with a bright green flip flop dangling from it. "I bought these, my pink ones are about knackered."

"I think you do it on purpose so you can buy some new shoes," I teased, "still, you've plenty of slippers at home."

"We're off for a game of bingo, are you coming?" enquired Greta.

"No thanks, I think we'll wander down to the amusements and fun fair," I replied.

"Okay, see you at the coach at six," called Greta. "Don't be late."

We ambled down to the amusement arcade and had a go on the 'slotties' which I hadn't done in years. I could hear the music from the fairground organ, which I loved – it usually accompanied the 'up and down' horses on the carousel. We soon found it and stood watching it as the beautifully painted horses rode round in front of us.

"Look!" Judy cried, pointing to the carousel. Riding sedately side by side were Doreen and Gladys! More and more of Doreen's rollers were protruding from her yellow head scarf. Somehow she had hitched her skirt up so high her stocking tops and suspenders were in full view.

"I didn't think women wore stockings and suspenders now," chuckled Judy.

"You would be surprised at what I have come across," I answered smiling.

"No I wouldn't - oh look, what is Gladys doing?" cried Judy

"As they passed us, Gladys stretched out her chubby legs in front.

"Whhee," she shouted with glee as her voluminous skirt blew up showing her huge white knickers to all and sundry.

"Come on let's go before they see us," I exclaimed.

We bought ourselves an ice-cream each and continued on our tour of the fun-fair.

"This looks good," said Judy, "we ought to have a go on something. Better finish our ice-creams first though."

Judy was talking about a ride on a waterway, taking you through a tunnel to different places in the world. Finishing our ices, we watched as boats floated gently by and waited until it was our turn.

We clambered into our boat and settled down to be transported sedately through the wonders of the world.

"I think it's time to go and grab a bite to eat before we head back to the coach," Judy suggested.

"Good idea, let's go," I agreed.

We arrived at the coaches with ten minutes to spare, and it looked as if most of the people were already back.

We climbed the steps into our coach and I glanced around smiling.

"Hi. Everybody had a nice day?" I enquired.

The consensus was that all had had a good day out. There were lots of red, sun caught faces and tired looking children.

"Who are we waiting for?" asked Greta, looking down the coach. "The rest are all back on the other two coaches."

"It's Doreen and Gladys," called Carol. "I saw them going in the pub as soon as we got here. Oh, it's okay, they are just coming."

"Thank God for that," muttered Greta, "come on you two, you're last again!"

Doreen and Gladys struggled up the steps and wobbled along the coach to their seats.

"We got pucked off the up and down porses. They said we were hissed and that Gladys was powing her knickers," announced Doreen with a very indignant expression on her face.

"Well, were you pissed?" asked Greta, grinning.

"I told you that I saw them going into a pub," said Carol.

"Be quiet, you snitch," growled Greta.

"We had a few lagers I suppose," sniggered Gladys, plonking herself down next to Doreen.

The journey home was quiet except for the loud snores of the two 'hissed' ladies.

CHAPTER 20

Mr Spence

The summer term arrived all too quickly. I introduced the Records of Achievement to the new Nursery intake and again they were received with enthusiasm. What a good idea they had been, forging such a close link between school and home.

The Maths, English and sewing classes continued to be well attended in the Room. Lizzie was in her last term of reading and writing classes, as were Janine and Jill with their Child Development course. Casey was continuing well with her counselling course and she and Ian were still attending Alcoholics Anonymous meetings.

Mr Spence, one of the new teachers, stopped me in the corridor. He explained that he was going to produce a monthly school newspaper, and did I know if any members of the Parents' Room would like to contribute?

"Why don't you come and ask them?" I said.

"Oh, I'm not sure about that," he stammered, looking worried.

"Come across at lunchtime, I'll be there. They don't bite," I smiled, "see you there."

I turned away before he could protest anymore. It was a busy morning, and Abbey and Sara were cooking spaghetti bolognese for everyone and I went out on a couple of home visits.

I had forgotten about Mr Spence when there was a knock on the Room door,

"Who's that? Nobody knocks to come in here," exclaimed Greta.

I suddenly remembered Mr Spence and rushed to open the door before he could escape.

"Hello, come in Mr Spence, how nice to see you," I enthused very tentatively.

Mr Spence came into the Room looking as if he was entering the Lions' Den and wishing the ground would swallow him up.

"Mr Spence is going to produce a school newspaper every month and he was wondering if any of you would like to contribute," I explained helping the poor man out.

"Hey, that's a good idea," exclaimed Casey, "I've been published already. I had a poem in the Gazette."

"Really, that's wonderful. I'm so pleased you think it's a good idea," he said, visibly relaxing.

"I'll have a go too," said Janine "sounds like fun."

"Me too," chipped in Sara, "and Abbey is great at drawing and art work."

"Something smells good," observed Mr Spence.

"It's spaggy bol, there's plenty if would like to stay and have lunch with us," offered Greta.

"Well, I don't know if I should really. Oh, why not? I'd love to stay, thanks," replied Mr Spence.

"Come and plonk your bum here next to me," said Carol, flashing her very best toothy smile, and patting the chair next to her.

"No, that's where I sit at lunchtime," said Greta, intervening, "you have my seat Mr Spence."

"Since when do you sit there at lunchtime?" hissed Carol.

"As from now," answered Greta through gritted teeth.

Lunchtime was lovely, and they discussed ideas for the newspaper. Mr Spence insisted on helping to wash up which earned him several Brownie points. Promising to come again soon, Mr Spence took his leave and I walked across the Hall with him.

"It's not at all like I was led to believe," he said. "I've really enjoyed that."

"Oh let me guess, the "disapproving gang" have been telling you all about the awful people and things that go on in there," I replied. "They criticise and complain, but they make no effort to come across just see what it is like."

"That's about it," said Mr Spence, "well, I know different now, thanks Sal – I can call you Sal, can't I?"

"Yes sure, Paul, isn't it?" I asked.

Paul nodded and smiled – he was really quiet cute.

"I shouldn't mind a bit of that," cried Carol as I went back into the Room, "he's fit, isn't he. I'll cook next time he comes."

"No you won't, you burn everything," grumbled Greta. "Now show some respect. Anyway, you've got a boyfriend."

"Oh him? He only comes round when he wants to get his leg over," muttered Carol.

"Too much info. be quiet," muttered Casey.

"We could do with some new books and toys in here," I said, changing the subject, "but there's not much money in the kitty at the moment."

"I could sell my body down the dock," cackled Carol

"That's enough of that now," I said sternly at Carol.

"You wouldn't make much," commented Casey, making everyone laugh.

"I've got an idea, but I don't know if we can manage it," said Emma.

"Go on, what is it?" I encouraged.

"Well, you know there is the Apple Blossom Care Home opposite the school. Why don't we do an Old Time Music Hall sing-song evening especially for them," continued Emma. "They could be guests of honour and anyone else who wants to come will pay fifty pence entrance fee."

"Oh gosh, I don't know about that," I replied, doubtfully.

"We could pick the most well-known songs and act them out, and sing all together," enthused Greta, her eyes glinting.

"Hang on Greta, didn't you sing in the pubs in Glasgow years ago?" I remembered.

"They were the days," said Greta, turning back the years. "I know most of the Music Hall songs but my favourite is a war time song called Keep the Home Fires Burning."

"Go on Greta, sing it for us now," pleaded Sara, "please."

The ciggie was carefully placed in an ashtray and Greta stood up.

Taking a deep breath she began to sing "keep the home fires burning," She had a deep, rich voice, a little grainy due to the many ciggies she smoked. She sang it with such passion and meaning there was silence in the room and all eyes were fixed on Greta.

I felt tears threatening to fall as the song came to an end. Greta opened her eyes and smiled to the applause. I think for a moment she was young again and back in the pubs of Glasgow.

"That was super," I gulped, "you've made me cry."

"You'll have to sing that on the evening," said Lizzie.

"Oh, so we are doing it then, are we?" I asked, "any excuse to get dressed up."

"It'll be fun," exclaimed Janine.

"We'll sort out our songs tomorrow shall we Sal?" asked Casey, her eyes shining at the thought.

"Okay, okay, I give in. Yes, we'll sort it tomorrow. I'll bring a list of songs in the morning," I chuckled. "Here we go again; I'd better run it past Mrs Harper."

"She'll love the idea," commented Emma.

CHAPTER 21

Old Time Music Hall

Mrs Harper loved the idea of course and offered to play the piano on the evening. The Apple Blossom Care Home was delighted to be invited, and would be bringing about thirty residents.

We had four weeks to get our act together and be ready for the big evening. Tickets had gone on sale to the parents of the school and were selling well. I really hoped we had not bitten off more than we could chew. Songs had been chosen, and for once rehearsals were being taken very seriously. For those who didn't want to sing on their own they were learning the words to sing along to a tape. Greta was singing 'My Old Man said Follow the Van' and "Keep the Home Fires Burning". Lizzie and Janine were singing 'The Sun has got his Hat On', and "Doing the Lambeth Waltz", and Casey and Emma were learning "Any Old Iron' and 'Where did you get that Hat.' Chris and Pete asked if they could sing 'If you were the only girl in the World'.

That left me with 'Waiting at the Church', I volunteered. "Perhaps Andy will sing it with me, Greta," I said.

"Andy's at work that night, sorry," explained Greta.

"Oh, okay, I'll sort something out, no worries," I replied.

Mr Spence had sorted out an overhead projector that showed the words of the songs so that everybody could join in. Sara was going to be in charge of that and Carol was looking after the refreshments at the interval with a couple of other parents.

Mr Spence had become a regular visitor to the Room especially on Thursday dinner day, and they all loved him.

"Hi Sal, a little bird told me that you are looking for a singing partner," he said. "How about me?"

"Oh no, really, I'll do it by myself, it'll be fine," I replied, feeling put on the spot.

"No, no, I insist. I can sing a bit you know," he replied with a cheeky grin. "Greta will be disappointed if I don't perform."

"If you have got Greta on your side, I don't stand a chance. Okay, thank you," I said, giving in gracefully.

I rehearsed with Paul a couple of times after school and he was right – he could sing. He had a lovely voice but I wasn't too bad myself, so our voices complimented each other.

The day of the concert arrived and there was great excitement and apprehension. Costumes were made and hung everywhere in the Room. I had kept my costume quiet, even from Paul. He was wearing a waistcoat with a ruffled white shirt and top hat. Casey and Emma were dressed in ragged clothes and caps for their rendition of 'Any Old Iron' and huge hats like Easter bonnets for 'Where did you get that hat?' Lizzie and Janine had long ball gowns for their song 'Doing the Lambeth Waltz', and huge sun hats for 'The sun has got its hat on' Greta had a lovely, long black sparkling dress. Pete was dressed in top hat and tails, and Chris was in a slim fitting, long ivory dress with a headband of pearls for their song 'If you were the only girl in the World'.

I decided that I had better get my costume on. It was a white wedding dress I had found in a second hand shop, plus a head-dress and veil. What I also did was to fasten two cushions round my waist, to make me look six months pregnant. I emerged from the toilet into the Room.

There was a moment of silence and then they all burst out laughing.

"Sal, that's great, how funny," chortled Casey, "you've been hiding that really well."

"Wait until Carol sees you. God know what she'll come up with," laughed Emma.

"Well look at you!" laughed Paul. "This will set tongues wagging."

Seven o' clock arrived and our guests from the care home began to arrive with their carers. Some came in wheel-chairs and some were able to walk unaided. They took up the first two rows and the rest of the audience sat behind them. The hall was just about full as seven thirty approached.

Mrs Harper welcomed everyone and the show began. Greta started with a fabulous rendition of 'Keep the home fires burning', her powerful voice filling the hall, and she finished to a rapturous round of applause. All of the acts did so well. Pete and Chris brought a tear to everyone's eyes who knew what a battle Chris had had with breast cancer – she really was Pete's 'only girl in the world'.

Then it was Paul's and my turn. We walked onto the stage amid laughter from the parents who knew us.

Then a familiar voice cackled out, "frigging hell. When did that happen?" Carol never failed to deliver.

The evening was a tremendous success, and we raised two hundred and fifty one pounds for new equipment for the Parents' Room and made a whole new set of friends from the Apple Blossom Care home.

CHAPTER 22
Final Countdown

"Anybody fancy earning a couple of quid extra?" announced Greta one day in July. "They are wanting people to pick cabbages down on the fens. You get taken in a coach and the pay isn't bad."

"Are you going Greta?" I asked, "it will be hard work."

I felt a little concerned it would be too much for her as she said herself that she was not a spring chicken any more.

"I thought I would give it a go as long as some others will go too," replied Greta. "It's Monday and Tuesday next week."

Casey, Janine, Emma, Lizzie and Abbey said that they would go as long as they could get some child care. Carol had no-one to look after Chloe, so she couldn't go – perhaps that was a good thing!

The Parents' Room was eerily quiet on the Monday morning as the girls were being picked up at seven in the morning from outside the chip shop. I had plenty of Nursery letters to deliver for the next intake, and I did wonder how they were getting on.

Carol and Chloe were keeping me company as I ate my lunch in the Room.

"I don't like this you know," said Carol, "it's too quiet."

"It does seem odd, I must agree," I nodded. "Still, it's only for a couple of days."

"I love coming in here," commented Carol. "I feel comfortable and safe, and I know there will always be somebody to talk to."

"Well, you'll have to make do with me today," I laughed.

"You're not like the other teachers though are you Sal?" she replied.

"How do you mean?" I asked.

"Well, we call you by your first name, you are more like one of us, you never look down on us, or looked shocked at anything we do or say," Carol said. "I guess what I'm trying to say is that you don't judge us like other people do."

That was quite a speech for Carol and I felt quite delighted at what she had said to me. I was just about to reply when she pointed out of the window

"What the frigging hell is going on, look?"

I looked out of the window and could see a small furniture van parked up in the Youth Centre car park near to the Parents' Room. On the side of the van was written Victor the Shifter. The back door of the van was open and there was Victor, I assume, helping Greta out of the van!! One by one the girls emerged from the van, giggling and laughing.

"What's happened do you think, Sal?" cried Carol.

"I've no idea, but we are about to find out," I answered laughing.

Victor drove out of the car park, waving out of the window at the girls, who were clapping and waving enthusiastically. They tumbled into the Room laughing and chattering loudly.

"Oh let me sit on the big easy chair, my back is killing me," announced Greta, "I need a fag."

"I'll put the kettle on and make the drinks," announced Carol.

"Good God, Carol making drinks. That's a first," exclaimed Casey. "You must have missed us!"

"No we haven't, have we Sal? We were having a nice quiet chat before you lot came back and disturbed us," replied Carol grinning and winking at me.

"If you say so Carol, but we were feeling a tad lonely really," I answered, "anyway, what happened?"

"It was Greta's fault," explained Emma. "The bloke wouldn't let her smoke whilst she was picking the cabbages."

"Well, I can understand that," I commented.

"Then he wouldn't let her have any more fag breaks," continued Lizzie.

"Yes, but to be fair, Greta wanted a fag break every ten minutes!" shrieked Janine, and they all fell about laughing. "Then Greta sat down and couldn't get up, and we were all laughing so much we couldn't help her, and then all of the rest of the work gang started to laugh too."

"Anyway, the bloke in charge picked Greta up and called her a stupid old faggot," continued Abbey, "so Greta picked up a cabbage and threw it at him, and it bounced off his head."

"He was so mad he ordered Greta to the coach and gave her the sack," chortled Casey. "Well, we decided that we couldn't have Greta tret like that so we all downed tools too."

"Oh Greta, what are you like?" I replied, chuckling at the story, "so what's with the furniture van?"

"We didn't want to wait for the coach home, it smelt funny anyway, so we walked to the main road and began to thumb for a lift," explained Greta. "We hadn't been thumbing long, when along came Victor. He drove past us at first and then came back as he is a friend of my Andy, and he recognised me. So we all piled into the back of his van. There were a few cushions to sit on, but it was a bit uncomfortable at first, but we had a good laugh."

Mrs Harper came into the room and looked astonished.

"I thought you were all picking cabbages," she exclaimed.

At this, they all dissolved into peals of laughter.

I knew that this story would be re-countered many times over the years to come.

The summer term was drawing to a close, and classes and courses coming to an end. Janine and Jill both passed their Child Development course and were so proud to be presented with their certificates by Mrs Harper in a school assembly. Everyone from the Parents' Room came into the assembly to share in their success. Lizzie asked if she could contribute an article for the school newspaper. It was called 'I learned to read and write'. How wonderful and brave of her to do that. I was invited to watch her receive her certificate of success, and much to my delight her mum was present too, looking proudly at her daughter.

Casey had another year to complete her counselling course and Abbey, Sara and Emma had signed up for Advanced Craft classes, and a Computer course. By going together they felt so much more self-confident.

Carol? Well Carol was Carol and there was no doubt she had flourished and grown. She was still reluctant to take part in any of the classes, but she did enjoy the talks, the bingo and generally being part of the group in the Parents' Room.

As for Greta, what can I say? She was a reliable stalwart in the Parents' Room and a highly respected member of the community. She had also become a very dear friend of mine.

"Are you ready Sal?" said a familiar voice, bringing me back abruptly from my memories. "You were miles away then,"

"It's been a long time since I was in here," I replied softly, not really wanting to be dragged away from my memories.

"My retirement party is over, so come on Mrs Spence, it's time to go home," replied my husband Paul. "Jenny will be home for the weekend from uni, and she'll be bringing a mountain of washing as usual."

"It's over twenty years since I left here, and I had Jenny a year after we got married," I reminded him.

"Yes, I got you to the church in the end," he answered smiling, "come on love, let's go."

As I walked out through the Parents' Room for the last time, I glanced round once more. They were all smiling at me – this wonderful group of people, and the wider school community that I had had the privilege of meeting, working with and making forever friends. There were far more memories that I had not had time to recall, but they are forever in my mind and in my heart – perhaps for another day.

Milton Keynes UK
Ingram Content Group UK Ltd.
UKHW040636041023
429927UK00001B/17

9 781803 815855